Diary of an A-Lister: Rising Star

C. L. Scott

ISBN:149954314X
ISBN-13: 978-1499543148

ACKNOWLEDGMENTS

Being able to continue with the series has been a wonderfully rewarding experience, and that is in no small part down to the support and insight of a few very important people.
Thank you once again to Liane for helping me to edit and shape the book in its final stages. You have an understanding of this world like no one else and it truly is a great help to have someone else see Rebecca's world through the same eyes as me.
To my Mum, who I know I can always turn to for honest advice, whether it be for the book or anything else. Your opinion is always my most sought after.
To James and Chris, for coming back on board, no questions asked, and creating another gorgeous front cover we can all be proud of.

And to everyone who bought the first book, who showed me their support by reading it (especially my Dad and brother!), and those who have pestered ever me ever since for the sequel - here it is. I hope you like it.

2002

JANUARY 5th

The glare of the lightbulbs around the mirror bathed me in a hazy glow as I sat staring at my reflection. Everything was perfect. My hair, make-up and wardrobe had been carefully planned and executed by the team and as I sat awaiting my call to the set, there was nothing else for me to do except sit, wait and panic.
"And on tonight's show, we have the sensational and incredibly beautiful star of the hit Young Bros. Network TV show, Davey's Crowd… That's Miss Rebecca Russo, everyone."
I glanced in the mirror at the TV hanging on the wall, its reflection showing the opening monologue of presenter Joey Cruz. He was calm, relaxed and

playing to the cameras, something I hoped I would be able to do in - quick glance at the clock – six minutes time.
My heart pounded heavily as I looked at the call-sheet that lay on the side, next to the fruit basket, bottles of water and cans of soda that had been left in the dressing room for me. I'd had a few sips of water but I wasn't in the mood to eat. My stomach was full of butterflies, anyhow. I picked up the call-sheet and looked at it.

THE LATE SHOW WITH JOEY CRUZ
FILMING BEGINS AT 16:00 HOURS

16:00 JOEY MONOLOGUE
16:05 MUSICAL SKETCH
16:08 COMMERCIAL BREAK
16:10 INTERVIEW - REBECCA RUSSO

I took a deep breath and exhaled, checking the clock again. Showtime was fast approaching…
I startled at the sound of raised voices on the other side of the door and heard the handle turning. A rush of backstage chatter filled the near silent room as Trish hurried in.
"You ready?"
I shrugged and gave a shaky smile.
"Ready as I'll ever be."
She smiled warmly at me and came over, giving me a pat on the shoulder.
"You'll be fine. I've run through the questions with the talent executive and the writers. There shouldn't be anything that catches you out."
I nodded, unsure that was really going to be the

case. Joey Cruz was known for asking hard, intrusive questions and having a wicked sense of teasing humour to go with it. He'd been polite and charming to me when he'd introduced himself about an hour ago, but I wasn't naïve enough to believe that he didn't have an off-screen persona that contrasted with his on-screen one. To say I was intimidated at this, my first late night talk show interview, would have been an understatement. But before my panic could spiral dangerously close to a full-blown attack, someone else came into the room wearing a headset and carrying a clipboard.

"Miss Russo, we're ready for you."

I looked at Trish with what must have been rabbit-in-the-headlights eyes. She lay a firm hand on my shoulder and leaned closer. Agent pep talk time.

"You're going to be fine," she assured. "The entire interview will be no more than eight minutes. You can do this."

I nodded, getting up from the chair and walking across the room. I pushed my shoulders back, ran my hands down my sleek brown hair and nodded at the lady.

"Follow me," she instructed.

We entered the corridor, which was bustling. People either stared at me or were too busy to care, and I followed the stage manager down the hall, which was lined with framed stills of past guests. They were all famous, recognisable faces, and I felt a pang of privilege knowing I was about to join the ranks of such stars. But as we entered the backstage area, the all-encompassing darkness surrounded us and fear coursed through my veins once more.

I concentrated on not tripping over any wires in the

dark, although the stage manager had helpfully turned on a torch and was shining it on the floor in front of my brand new high-heeled shoes. I glanced ahead and saw the light of the set peeking through from behind a tall curtain. Just the other side of that curtain was Joey Cruz, his house band, about 200 audience members and a whole host of cameras, ready to beam me into TV sets around the country. I felt sick.

I turned to Trish but I knew it was too late. Too late for any wise words of wisdom, too late for a quick dash to the bathroom, and definitely too late to back out. The stage manager held a radio to her mouth and spoke, though I couldn't hear it above the introductory saxophone music being played by the band just inches from me on the other side of the curtain.

"Please welcome our special guest, Rebecca Russo!"

The stage manager stepped back and held out her arm. This was happening. This was my life, right now. I forced myself to put one foot in front of the other, climbed the three steps to stage level and walked out from behind the curtain.

The spotlights were on me, which made it hard to see anything much at all. But I knew where the seats were, where Joey was, and turned my body instinctively in that direction. The walk looked like miles and the floor was so shiny, I began to dread how slippery it might be, and slowed my pace a little to compensate. The last thing I needed was to arrive at Joey's side via a sliding baseball-style run on my ass.

There he was. Not knowing what the interview was going to be like, in that moment, Joey was my only

friend. I glanced towards the audience, whom I could just about make out, but instead saw all the cameras pointed right at me. Focus on Joey, I instructed myself, and he held out his hand to me as I finally reached the chairs.
He shook my hand warmly and smiled at me. "Great to see you."
"Thank you," I said, shaking his hand before he let go and made his way back to his seat behind the desk. I looked down at the two chairs, side by side, and of course went for the one closest to him. I sat down, brushing my hands underneath my dress as I did so, and crossed my legs. I'd made it.
I turned my body towards Joey and smiled, taking a deep breath I hoped no one would see.
"Welcome to the show," Joey said, as the band struck their final drum beat. I smiled warmly.
"Thank you for having me," I said, thinking how proud my Mom would be of my polite manners.
"So it's 2002, the start of a brand new year. Have you made any New Year's resolutions?" Jeyed asked.
"Uh, no, not really."
"You're just perfect in every way?" he remarked with a quirked, challenging eyebrow. Really? Already? I took a breath, a pause, just as Trish had advised, letting my thoughts settle into a cohesive response.
"Far from it," I said, pushing my hair behind my ears. "I've just been so busy I haven't really thought much about it."
"Busy, you say? Is that filming Davey's Crowd?" The audience roared into applause and I felt boosted by their support. I grinned and nodded.

"Yes. We're just starting the second half of the third season."
"Now this show, right, the way I see it…it's just incredibly popular."
I nodded proudly as he continued.
"Why do you think that is? I mean, besides the fact that you're all great to look at."
The audience laughed, as did I, and I lay my hands gracefully in my lap.
"I think we have some fantastic writers on the show, who really get what growing up and being a teenager is all about. And they frame that reality in what I suppose is like, a heightened version of that. A lot of what we do on the show, of course, wouldn't happen in real-life but at its core, the characters are real. The relationships and emotions are real…"
Excellent waffle, I commended myself, but I'd run out of it. I glanced at Joey. He nodded.
"You say things that 'wouldn't happen in real-life'. Such as what?"
"Well, on next week's episode, we're all stuck in a bomb scare at the mall."
Joey nodded thoughtfully. Or mock-thoughtfully, anyway.
"Those things happen," he deadpanned. This was hard. I nodded.
"Well, of course, but the likelihood of having all the principal cast members at the mall, at the same time…and there's lots of drama, like the mall itself is hosting a child beauty pageant, so there's all these helpless little kids there too, you know, so…"
Praying he would help me out just a little, Joey sat back in his chair and crossed his arms.

"So does the bomb go off?"
I flashed him a smile.
"Perhaps," I shrugged, glancing towards the audience. "You'll just have to tune in to find out."
The audience applauded and Joey sat forward again.
"Promoted like a seasoned professional," he said in half-compliment, half-snidey remark. "Which in a way you are, being the daughter of Millie and Dan Russo."
The audience launched into excitable cheering which wasn't unexpected, but still felt a bit awkward. Hollywood mega-couple that they were, they were also just my parents after all.
"What was it like growing up in a showbiz family? I mean, your older brother David is an actor, and your sister Stacey too..."
More cheers. More cringing. I could only shrug.
"It's weird for me because you know, they're just my family. And I know we're all on TV, or in the movies, but we're still just a regular family."
Joey practically scoffed and for the first time in the interview, I began to actually dislike him. There was no need to be rude.
"I can imagine the Russo's fighting over the remote. 'No, no, *I* want to be on the TV!'" he teased, and the audience laughed. I felt my defences rising. If there was one thing that ignited my fierce loyalty, it was my family.
"All our egos get checked at the door," I explained calmly. "My parents have never made us feel like we're anything out of the ordinary, or exceptional, or anything like that."
"So they're not supportive?"

Now he was just twisting my words.
"*No,*" I returned, trying not to let my anger reveal itself in the tone of my voice. "Quite the opposite. They're incredibly supportive. They've always backed us 110% percent."
"So they're pushy parents then?" Joey challenged. "I mean, we see that all the time in Hollywood, don't we?"
He held his hand out towards the audience, inviting their shared support. No way, they're *my* audience, I thought.
"You went to a drama school, right, in Philadelphia, instead of a normal high school? So they were pushing you down this path right from the start?"
"I went to the Philadelphia High School for Creative and Performing Arts," I clarified, now determined to prove myself to be gracious in the face of attack, "which means yes, we took classes on acting, singing, dancing, that kind of thing. But we also had to study regular subjects and pass our GED tests just like everyone else."
Joey nodded. He clearly knew nothing about this, or me, and I'd just schooled him. I sat up a little straighter in my seat, a little more confidently. Ha.
"Now I believe it was at high school that you met your recently estranged ex-boyfriend Josh Parker, is that correct?"
Damn it. He did know all about me after all. I felt my cheeks flush and my heart begin to race. My personal life was next to be critiqued. I nodded in confirmation.
"So you guys were high school sweethearts?" Joey smiled. I smiled and nodded again.
"Yes, we were."

"I bet you were Prom Queen too..."
It wasn't flirting, nor was it a compliment. The sly smile on his face was etched with resentment. But hell, I was proud of being Prom Queen, so I nodded and smiled brightly.
"Right again," I charmed.
"But you guys aren't together anymore?"
I slumped my shoulders a little, without even realising.
"Isn't that hard? Breaking up with someone but still having to work with them? I mean, you two still have to play a couple on the show, right?"
"Yes, we do," I nodded, squirming in my seat. "But we still have a really good working relationship, a good relationship overall really, so it's fine."
"A little birdie told me that a certain Mr Riley Kitson might have had something to do with your split..."
This was what he'd been building up too. This was what I knew, deep down, everyone in the audience and at home were waiting to hear about. Not my TV success, not my upcoming projects, not even getting a little insight into the real me (albeit in rushed talk-show format), no - they all wanted to know about my hook-up with Hollywood bad boy Riley Kitson.
I paused, forced a smile and slowly nodded my head. The audience whooped and cheered. It was weird. They didn't know anything about us - how could they be so happy about us being together?
Joey nodded, taking a moment. I absolutely dreaded his next question.
"So it is love?"
That threw me. I suddenly had an image of Riley

watching on TV at home. What would he want me to say? What would he expect me to say? I wished I'd taken Trish's advice - paused, regained my composure, figured out something smart to say - but instead my mouth engaged before my brain and I began to ramble nervously, live on TV.
"I, uh…I mean, really that's just…it's really very early to be throwing around words like...*love*."
"So it's all about the sex then?"
The audience gasped and laughed and I felt like the entire room, the entire country, were now picturing us having sex. I wanted to *die*.
"Come on!" Joey defended himself with a cocky smile. "She's 18 now! And he's a good-looking guy!"
I smiled sardonically at Joey, who flashed me a 'got ya' grin right back. I raised an eyebrow and stared him out, waiting for the audience noise to die down.
"So it is?" he taunted.
"My private life is exactly that. Private."
He clapped his hands together, clearly seeing that as a win.
"I think we all know what *that* means, don't we everyone?"
The audience laughed. They were clearly not on my side anymore. This felt like the Middle Ages. I half-expected to be led to the stocks to have rotten vegetables thrown at me. How humiliating. I had to try to get this interview back somehow.
"Listen," I said, leaning forwards, and Joey hushed the audience by waving his arms. "Riley and I have just started seeing each other and it's going well."
Joey nodded. I realised I didn't have anything else

to say. My words just hung awkwardly in the air for what seemed like forever. Joey nodded slowly. "O-kay then," he said, extending the awkwardness. "Moving on… Your next project."
The sudden change in subject threw me and I struggled to remember what it was even called.
"Irresponsible Actions," I said with a smile, and he raised an eyebrow, looking towards the audience. Oh ha ha, I thought. How childish.
"And that's not with Riley Kitson, no…?" he smirked.
"No," I replied. "I'm actually starring opposite Oliver Rose."
"That British kid? From the Crusader movies?"
An image of the poster for Teen Crusader flashed in my mind, Oliver Rose decked out in sword-fighting Robin Hood-style garb. That franchise had made him a worldwide heartthrob overnight.
"Yes," I confirmed with a nod. Joey leaned conspiratorially forwards.
"Rebecca?"
"Yes?" I leaned closer, playing along.
"He's a handsome guy."
"Yes, he is."
"More handsome than say…Riley Kitson?"
"Not in my opinion," I returned and the audience 'oohed'. This was feeling more and more like a pantomime the longer it went on.
"So no chance of an office romance, then?"
"I doubt it," I smiled, sitting back in my chair.
"Well, how about we agree that you come back on the show for our Valentine's Day episode and we'll see who your hunky Valentine is then, huh?"
The audience erupted into whistles and cat-calls

and applause and I smiled at Joey, giving him a nod. I hoped that wasn't a binding contract - if I never set foot on this set again, it would be a day too soon.
"Well, good luck with the new movie, the show, your love life…" (audience laughter) "Rebecca Russo, everybody!"
There was a final round of rapturous applause as Joey looked down the camera that had come hurtling towards us and said,
"We'll be right back after these commercials."
The band started up and Joey held out his hand. I shook it and politely smiled but squeezed his hand just a little more tightly this time. What a jerk.
"Rebecca, thank you," he said, as the crew began busying themselves again, setting up for after the break. I stood up as the stage manager came towards me.
"Thank you, that was great," I replied charmingly to Joey, showing him some real acting prowess. I even gave him a wave as I walked off set. The audience gave me a parting half-hearted round of applause but they weren't in my good books - how fickle the masses could be, I realised. Most of them were probably fans and yet they were happy to see me embarrassed on national TV for entertainment purposes.
Trish was waiting for me and as I looked at her, I pulled a dejected face. She shook her head and put her arm around me as we followed the stage manager back to the dressing room.
"You did great."
I leaned away and looked at her.
"Really?"

"Really," she said soothingly. "That was your first live interview and Joey is notoriously tricky."
"I'll say," I said, rolling my eyes. "It felt more like a battlefield than a talk show."
The stage manager stopped at the door, opened it then stood to one side. She smiled at me.
"She's right," she said, nodding at Trish. "You handled yourself pretty well up there against Joey."
"You really think so?"
She nodded.
"It's your first time. You'll get better."
I sure hoped so, I mused, as I went into the dressing room and straight over to my bag. My phone was ringing and I fished it out, pausing to check the display. 'RILEY'. My heart quickened, for various reasons, as I held it to my ear.
"Hello?"
"Hey baby."
The sound of his deep, sexy drawl both soothed me and thrilled me. Then I remembered the interview.
"What did you think?" I asked tentatively.
"You did real good."
"You sure? I mean, you weren't mad about what I said…"
"Why would I be mad?"
"Because…" I said, tailing off. I hadn't said I loved him. It was stupid, I realised, being as we'd only been together for a few months. And we hadn't actually said it to each other privately, let alone blurting it out for the first time on TV. But still. It wasn't like I didn't feel really strongly about him, or that I wasn't happy in our relationship. And I didn't want him to think that.
"He put you in a difficult position and you handled

it well," Riley reasoned.
"So long as we're cool," I said, glancing in the mirror.
"We're cool," he replied, and I watched myself smile.
"Well, good."
"And I just gotta say...you looked hot."
My smile turned into a grin.
"I mean...*hot*," he reiterated, and my heart skipped a beat. I glanced at myself in the mirror. This dress did cling to my body in all the right places. And whatever high-shine product they'd put on my hair made it almost sparkle in the light.
"Well...thank you," I hushed back, aware that this private moment was being overheard by Trish, who was at least pretending to busy herself by rummaging through the contents of her handbag.
"When can I see you?" Riley asked.
"I don't know," I purred down the phone, running my finger along the back of the chair, "When's your next break in filming?"
"Saturday."
I rolled my eyes.
"We've got an all-nighter Saturday, I know it. We just got the schedule."
"Do you think your people could get in touch with my people and we could try and sync these schedules up somehow?"
"Wouldn't that be ideal," I replied in a sarcastic tone, knowing just how perfect that scenario would be for us. It didn't help that we were both working actors, but having his show, Hazy Days, shooting in Los Angeles and mine all the way across the country in Massachusetts was making seeing each

other almost impossible.
"Well, when I *do* get to see you again," he said, as I imagined his sultry smirk on the other end of the line, "maybe we can give Joey Cruz something to hang his wild theories on."
"Oh really?" I played along. The nature of our long-distance and practically non-existent relationship had meant finding an opportunity to spend some time together on a 'one-to-one basis' hadn't actually happened yet. The longer it went on, the more I anticipated it, and the more I anticipated it, the more I craved it.
"I'll just have to be content with watching re-runs," he sighed.
"Of the interview? Oh God, no one needs to be reliving that again."
Riley laughed.
"No, I meant Davey's Crowd."
"You've been watching my show?" I smiled, my heart skipping a happy beat.
"Well, how else am I going to get to see you?"
I shrugged to myself.
"If only you had, I don't know, *one* episode without Josh being in it..."
I nodded understandingly.
"I know, I know..."
"I mean, *is* there an episode? Because I would TiVo that shit like, right now."
I paused, looking up at the ceiling. Was there an episode without Josh in it? Jonny was a principal character but still... I shook my head.
"I don't think there is, sorry."
"Do the writers have any desire to kill him off?"
"Riley!" I scolded.

"His character, I mean!" he protested.
"I know…"
If Riley really was watching old re-runs of Davey's Crowd, then it must have been a pretty torturous experience for him, seeing his girlfriend making out with her ex-boyfriend on screen. Like, *a lot*. That was sort of Casey and Jonny's thing, the excessive PDA's.
"Well, I assure you," I said, "that arranging my schedule to include some one-on-one Riley Kitson time is my top priority."
"It had better be," he flirted, and I imagined his handsome face smiling that sexy smirk of his and I knew that if it hadn't been before, seeing him again really *was* my new top priority.
"Until then," he said.
"Until then," I agreed, with a daydreamy kind of sigh. I hung up the phone and put it back in my bag. I looked at Trish and we shared a smile.
"You ready to go?" she asked.
I nodded and followed her out of the dressing room. People said goodbye and nice to see you and waved us off, but I was glad to be out of there, truth be told. We got into a waiting car and shut the doors, Trish giving them the address to my Manhattan apartment. Would Steph be there when I got back? Or Seth? I knew Josh wouldn't be - he was still in Lexington filming scenes for the show. I would be back there this time tomorrow, probably standing opposite him spewing well-written verbal attacks in the scripted dance that was Jonny and Casey's on-off relationship. I smiled. I knew how lucky I was to be on that show, and to still count Josh as not only a fantastic co-star but as a good

friend. He'd made my life a whole lot easier by not holding a grudge. And it also meant we'd both retained the right to stay in our dream-come-true New York apartment following our break-up.
I gazed out of the window and watched the city rush by, a blur of yellow taxis, bleak but busy sidewalks and the occasional flash of an illuminated billboard. New Yorkers were busy, self-absorbed people, and I loved them for that. I got to be largely anonymous when I was here, on account that people rarely bothered to give me the time of the day. I liked it that way, because being an actress didn't exactly go hand in hand with being left alone.
We stopped outside my apartment and I noticed some people milling around by the doors. This was a new thing, which I presumed had something to do with the increased tabloid coverage following my hook-up with Riley. We always had fans hanging around on set but crowds loitering by my front door was definitely a new, and not entirely welcome, thing.
I climbed out of the car and headed towards the building. I smiled politely and watched as everyone turned to stare at me. Unsure of quite what to do, I reached into my bag for my keys.
"Can we have your autograph?" someone asked.
"Sure," I smiled, taking the 'Teen Talk' magazine and the pen and signing my name right across the cast picture of Josh, Meghan, Jared, Connor and I - my Davey's Crowd family.
Handing it back, I scanned their expectant, nervous faces. Three girls, two guys.
"Can I have a picture with you, please?" one of the

girls asked, and I obliged, smiling into the lens as I was becoming so used to.
"Thank you so much!" she gushed, her face pink and her eyes wide. I smiled back.
"Not a problem."
Trish had joined me and had managed to get past them and round to the door. She pulled it open and stood, waiting patiently but also offering me a way out.
"I really have to go," I said apologetically, and they turned to look at Trish. Better to make her the bad guy, I supposed. I squeezed between them, giving them a smile and a wave, when one of the guys thrust a photograph at me. It was from my racy spread for Express magazine. I was stretched out across a scattering of fluffy cushions, wearing a pretty (but also pretty revealing) set of underwear, a sexy smile and not a lot else. I glanced at the man, who was simply staring expectantly back at me. I blushed, quickly signed my name and handed it back. How awkward to think he had that picture of me, and that was how he saw me - or rather *could* see me - whenever he wanted. Ironic considering my actual boyfriend hadn't even seen me that way yet. But such was the nature of the business, and sexy photo-shoots went hand in hand with difficult talk show interviews, postponed movie shoots and crowds of strangers hanging around outside your apartment. Trish flashed me a grin as I stepped past her.
"Welcome to the world of being famous," she said, with a smile.

JANUARY 15TH

I closed the door behind us and locked it. Josh lingered as I put my keys into my bag and zipped up my coat as I struggled to put the rucksack onto my back.
"Need any help there?" he asked, just as I got it sorted.
"Nah, I'm good."
"God, I'm hungry," he grumbled, as he set off down the stairs, and I rolled my eyes in response. He turned in time to see them and nodded, patting his stomach.
"I know, I know. You did offer me the pancake opportunity of a lifetime."
"And as usual, you turned them down only to wish you hadn't all of, ooh…" I said, checking my watch, "fifteen minutes later."
He paused as we reached the bottom of the stairs and did a quick bow, to which I nodded and smiled

courteously.
"Once again, your knowledge of me astounds," he quipped.
"Once again," I returned, as we stepped outside the apartment building, "your eternally-grumbling stomach is our focus of attention."
Josh stopped and raised his eyebrow.
"Ouch. Someone's sharp this morning."
I smiled.
"Just getting into character," I commented, and he smiled back at me.
"Then so shall I," he announced. "Would Miss Bridges care to accompany Mr Simms to the grocery store so he can cease his growling mid-regions?"
"Of course," I smiled up at Josh, as I linked my arm with his and we strode along the street together, arm in arm.
It was surprisingly bright and sunny for a January morning. The sun was most definitely up but its warming qualities were only vaguely noticeable compared to its eye-squinting glare. We turned towards the store, checking the traffic as we crossed the street, and I shivered as the cool wind grazed my cheeks unrelentingly.
"Jeez, it could warm up by a few degrees, surely?"
"It *is* January, my dear," Josh replied in a British accent, and I nodded as we continued.
"Too true."
We walked into the store, where Josh grabbed a bag of tortillas and a can of Coke. I commented on his unusual and somewhat disgusting choice (how could I not?!) to which he gave me a pained expression, fake of course, before handing over a

ten dollar bill. I raised a dismissive hand in his direction as we exited the store.

***

"Whassup, my homies?!" Connor called as we neared the hustle and bustle of set. I waved as a couple of assistants came dashing over and steered me towards my trailer.
"You're late," one of them said, as I waved goodbye to Josh.
"Sorry. Josh had to grab some breakfast."
"It's okay," another said. "Meghan hasn't arrived yet either."
"She's perfecting the fashionably late entrance," I smiled as we climbed the steps and headed inside the warm trailer. Ah, my little home from home. I took off my coat and placed it on the sofa as they began to open their make-up chests and go over the script details.
Just as we'd begun with foundation and brushing my hair, there was a knock at the door. Caroline opened the door, where Alonzo, our set costume supervisor, was waiting.
"Hey Al," I smiled, "How's it going this morning?"
"Good, thanks. How's our number one star doing?"
"I don't know. You'll have to ask Jared that," I joked, and he grinned, indicating the moveable rail of clothes beside him.
"Got your first and second outfits here," he said to Caroline. "Where d'ya want them?"
"Just bring them in and we'll hang them up over there," she pointed, and Alonzo brought the plastic-covered ensembles inside and hung them up.

"If anything doesn't fit..."
"Call you," I finished, and he nodded, pointing at me as he left.
"See you on set," he said, as I called a goodbye to him and let the hair and make-up assistants get me ready.

***

Later that morning, I was filming a scene with Josh and Jared.
"Okay, and we want you two to come in from over there," our director Lance indicated, and Josh and I nodded. "You're holding hands, you're talking and smiling about something. Then as the camera moves in, you start with the dialogue."
He did this with huge, sweeping arm gestures and we both nodded in understanding. We were three seasons in now; there was definite short-hand to all this.
"And then you come to here," he pointed, almost to where we were already standing, "and stop. That's when Jared comes in."
We both instinctively glanced at Jared, who was having his face brushed with make-up. A somewhat easygoing kind of relationship had returned between the boys, now that Jared was keeping his ego in check and Josh had learnt to forgive and be the bigger man. But they were far from being the buddies they'd once been back in the first season. Still, I had my own dynamic with Josh to be concerned with - I didn't have time to worry about anyone else's.
"Okay, let's get this show on the road," Josh

declared, clapping his hands together.
I followed him down the high school corridor set towards the doors. Extras were milling about, some of them watching us, and we came to a stop. I looked at Josh.
"You ready?" he asked.
I nodded and we turned to look at Lance. Josh slid his hand into mine and I glanced at it before looking up at him. We shared a smile that told each other this was okay again now. We could do this and have it not be weird.
"Okay…markers," Lance called out, and the extras seemed to stop and settle into position. "And background."
They started to move and I took a deep breath, focussing my brain on my first line.
"Roll camera…and, action!"
Josh and I set off at a slow, easy pace, reciting our scripted banter word perfectly.
"CUT!"
Everyone slowed to a stop and turned to look at Lance.
"Start again, but without holding hands," he said, and we hurried back to our starting point. The same instructions were called, we set off and repeated our lines. This time we got all the way to the next point, outside the classroom, when Lance yelled cut again.
"Try that line again, Beccy, but without the smile. A little smile to yourself, but not at Josh."
I nodded and glanced at Lance, then Josh, waited for 'Action' and obeyed. Another exchange was completed before Lance was interrupting again. This time, I lowered my eyes and Josh let out a

gentle sigh.
"What did you do now?" he teased me, and I flashed him a playful glare.
"No, no, there wasn't anything wrong," Lance said, coming towards us. "I just wanted to…"
He gently moved Josh and I apart then stood back, glancing around us, clearly sizing up the framing for the shot in his mind. He shook his head.
"No, it was fine as it was. As you were," he mumbled, walking back to the camera and taking a look at the display. I sneaked a look at Josh, who wide-eyed me with a hint of a grin, before raising his hand to cover his mouth.
"I can see this is going to be a *long* morning," he muttered and I smiled politely, risking a glance at Lance, who was chatting animatedly to his assistant director, before giving Josh a proper smile as I pushed my hair behind my ears.
"Okay, from the top!" Lance called, and Josh and I trudged along the hall and back to position one. Again.
As we approached the doorway, I turned to Josh and he to me.
"So do you really think you're going to last all morning without me?" he smirked.
"I can but try," I teased with a smile, holding my hand to my forehead, feigning the pain of being apart.
We grinned at each other as he tugged on my hand and pulled me close. I closed my eyes and tilted my face towards him as his lips met mine. I felt his hand slide onto my face, underneath my hair, and pull me deeper into his kiss. It was at times like these when the lines between Josh and I, and Casey

and Jonny, began to blur. But then...
"Cut!"
We opened our eyes and pulled apart, both looking instinctively towards Lance, who gave us a thumbs up. Josh and I smiled at each other and the scene was finally in the can.

***

"So how long have you actually been doing this for?" Sara asked. Being one of the two new cast members this season, she was keen on asking a lot of questions. But I liked her, so I didn't mind answering them, especially as we were both waiting for a lighting rig to go up. Huddled together in our matching puffa coats, clutching cups of coffee, who knew how long it would be before we filmed our final scene of the evening.
"Almost three years now," I replied in response to her question.
She wide-eyed me and nodded.
"Do you still enjoy it?"
"Oh, absolutely. It's still as much fun, if not more so, than when we started. We're all so close now that it's just a completely good time guaranteed, no matter who you have scenes with. We used to be a little more wary around each other to begin with, when we were still getting to know each other."
"I can see that," she nodded. "How close you are, I mean. You, Jared, Josh, Meghan...you've had a lot of people come and go, haven't you?"
I nodded and smiled.
"Yeah, we're just part of the furniture now..."
She began shaking her head apologetically and I

smiled.
"I was..."
"I know," I grinned. "I know what you meant. But yeah, we have. Obviously Connor is a regular now, but he didn't join 'til halfway through season one. And we've had some new people join since then, like you..."
Sara's cool. Okay, so she's like, 26, which makes her a whole eight years older than me, but she's down-to-earth and fun to be around. She rags on Josh a lot, and they love to catch each other out and tease each other, which is fun to watch.
"So have you and Josh always been a couple?" Sara asked.
I raised my eyebrows over the top of my cup of coffee.
"Woah, way to change the subject."
She smiled awkwardly at me but kept her gaze firm.
"No," I answered. "We met on the show. But he transferred to my high school at the same time, so it was like, double whammy."
"And did you hook up right away?"
"Pretty much," I nodded. "I was sort of seeing someone at the time..."
I wasn't going to name drop Lane Deacon if I could help it. Sara's head might have popped clean off her shoulders. He was, after all, our generation's biggest heartthrob and award-winning actor all rolled into one.
"To tell you the truth, I kind of liked Jared first."
Sara was intrigued by this, I could tell. Her eyes went all wide and goggly.
"I mean, we pretty much had all our scenes

together in the first season, and we got on like a house on fire," I explained.
"So what changed?"
I shrugged then smiled, my mind filling with Josh's grinning face.
"Josh just totally won me over. The more I got to know him, the more I liked him. We started hanging out at school too, and we were part of this big group of friends, and everyone was hooking up into couples and basically….yeah. That was that."
Sara smiled and I did too.
"So I broke up with…uh," I stumbled, trying to smooth over Lane's name, "my boyfriend at the time and started going out with Josh. And here we are. Or *were*, I should say."
Sara nodded more seriously.
"How is it working together?"
"And living together," I added and she paused thoughtfully then nodded. She knew this. I shrugged again.
"It's okay, I guess. I mean, it could have been so much harder. I honestly don't know what I would have done if he hadn't let me make the decisions I made and just let things be between us. I mean, we still really care about each other. So that's good."
"But you're with Riley Kitson now, right?"
I didn't even have time to register the smile that spread across my face before it was already a beaming grin. I caught Sara's eye and she smiled.
"I take it things are going well between you two, judging by the size of that smile on your face."
I giggled and she did too, and I took a sip of my coffee as I paused for thought. The simple answer was yes. Things were fine. But then again, I hadn't

seen him in weeks. And we barely had time to even speak on the phone due our hectic (and apparently clashing) work schedules. We were constantly missing each other and having to leave voicemails. But every time I played one back and heard his deep, sexy voice on the other end of the line, my heart would skip a beat and I knew how I really felt about him. I could only hope he felt the same way as me.
Before my mind could wander into negative and anxiety-ridden territory, Sara and I were called on set and it was time to shoot the scene.

***

Talking to Sara about Riley had sent me into a stress spiral. By the time I stopped by Josh's trailer at half past midnight, I was so deep inside my own head I barely even registered his hello. He waved his hand in front of my face and I looked up at him.
"Sorry," I mumbled, shaking my head.
"Jeez, Beccy, Planet Earth calling," he said, shutting the door to his trailer behind him and hopping down the steps. We both walked together in silence. He nudged my elbow.
"Everything okay?"
I looked at him and saw the concerned expression on his face. I shook myself out of my mood and nodded brightly.
"Uh huh."
He knew I was faking.
"You know you can tell me, right? Whatever's going on with you..." he said, a few moments later.
My fake smiled faded and I searched his eyes. He

was being open and honest with me - but could I do the same with him? Ordinarily, yes, but in this case, no. I lowered my gaze and watched my feet padding along the sidewalk. Josh said goodnight to one of the security guards but that was the only noise that cut through the quiet still of the night.
"Seriously, Beccy, what's wrong? I hate to see your face like that," he said, reaching over to take hold of my chin in his hand. He turned it towards him and pouted.
"So sad," he frowned and I pulled my head free of his grasp.
"I can't talk to you about this."
"Is it a girly thing?" he asked, screwing up his nose. I couldn't help but smile.
"In a way, yes."
Unfounded self-doubt was definitely a girly thing.
"And it doesn't have anything to do with us?"
I looked at him and shook my head.
"No," I replied firmly. He nodded and looked ahead as we crossed the empty street.
"I just..." he said, blowing on his fingers as he clasped them together next to his lips. "I figured we could talk about anything."
I sighed.
"Please don't make me tell you about this. You really don't want to know. I just need you to be...*you*."
Josh looked at me and we stopped walking.
"What does that mean?"
"I mean," I mumbled, "just...sweet. And supportive. And there for me. No questions asked." I looked at him when I said that last part, willing him to stop asking me said questions. Josh looked

back, searching my eyes with his own. I think he was savouring the barrage of compliments I'd just paid him. He sniffed and nodded and put the key into the door, letting us into the building.
When we finally got inside the apartment, after taking off our coats, he surprised me by pulling me into a hug. As I settled into it and held him tightly, the surprise faded and was replaced by the content feeling I always got from a Josh hug.
"I know it's about Riley," he said.
I tensed up and he pulled away, looking down at me. He smiled gently.
"It's okay. I'm not jealous anymore."
"You're not?" I asked.
"No," he said. "I was actually thinking we have something that transcends a normal relationship. Something way more special."
I gazed up into his eyes as they looked lovingly down onto me. I couldn't argue with that. Whatever we had been, and whatever we were now, definitely wasn't a normal relationship. I squeezed him one more time and thanked my lucky stars for that.

FEBRUARY 14TH

I'm coming to see you.

That was the message I'd received from Riley just two days ago. I picked up the phone almost immediately and called him to find out what was going on. He was coming into New York for the Valentine's Day weekend and thank God I wasn't working. So we decided, or rather he decided, it was high time we went on a 'proper' date. I couldn't contain my excitement and my ever-present life companion Josh was first to sense a change in me.

"You've been somewhere else all afternoon," he remarked, as we stood choosing our lunch from the craft service selection. I picked up a muffin and put it on my plate with a smile.

"It's...nothing," I said, apparently still trying to be sensitive towards him, even after all this time.

"Is it Riley-related?"

I looked over at him. The reality of the situation

was I'd moved on. I had a new boyfriend. I couldn't play this tip-toeing role any more. And besides, Josh should be used to it by now.
"Yes," I nodded, "He's coming to New York this weekend."
He nodded himself and reached for a bag of chips. "So you're finally getting to see him then? It's been quite a while, hasn't it?"
"New Year's Eve," I said quietly, recalling how awkward that night had been, for all three of us.
Josh opened his bag of chips and popped one in his mouth with a crunch.
"Well…" he began, before pausing. Apparently he didn't know quite what to say. He looked at me.
"Have fun," he said.
To anyone else, his smile and his words would have seemed sincere. But I knew him too well.
As soon as my final scene wrapped, I was back to the apartment in a flash, packing up a few things, grabbing my phone charger and my handbag. Josh was thankfully still on set so there was no need for a sort-of-sincere goodbye. We have unlimited use of a private car service (thank-you Young Bros.) so I jumped into the pre-booked car and happily sat back in the seat, watching as Lexington became a distant memory.
Three hours later, we were pulling up outside my other apartment, the bigger, nicer one, with the New York skyline view. I'd never been so happy to be home. As I slid the key into the front door, I realised I didn't even know if Steph or Seth were home.
"Hello?" I called out.
There was a pause, then a muffled reply.

"Hello?"
Seth. I closed the door behind me and carried my things towards the stairs. Seth appeared at the top, smiling down at me curiously.
"What are you doing here?"
"I live here, remember? Duh…" I said, before flashing him a cheeky smile.
"I mean," he said, twisting one of his metallic blue hair spikes between his fingers as he always did (bad habit), "how come you didn't say?"
"It was sort of a last minute thing," I explained, reaching the tops of the stairs, dropping my bag and giving him a hug.
"Riley's in town," I said with a wide grin as I pulled away. Seth quirked an eyebrow.
"Do you need the apartment? Because I can make myself scarce."
I paused, my heart in a constricted knot. Did I? Would I? Riley and I were finally going to see each other, and our agenda definitely wasn't to sit sweetly holding hands and reciting poetry to each other. My heart raced. Would tonight be the night?
"Uh," I said, pushing my hair behind my ears (bad habit), "I…honestly don't know."
"Ah, c'mon," Seth grinned. "The dude's not flying across the country for conversation."
"Where's Steph?" I asked, desperate to change the subject.
"She had this thing to go to."
I nodded.
"Is she back later?"
"Uh, no, she's not. It's a photo-shoot thing. Apparently it might go on for a while," Seth said, glancing down the stairs.

"Okay, cool," I nodded, picking up my bag. I thumbed in the direction of my bedroom, he nodded down the stairs at me, and we parted. Seth and I got on well, but we were still in that dynamic of 'best friend's boyfriend/girlfriend's best friend', which meant conversation was usually a little limited. I went into the bedroom and flopped on the bed.

Well, if tonight was the night, then it was time for a full-scale make-over.

***

I emerged from the bathroom half an hour later ready in body but far from ready in mind. Okay, so Riley was my boyfriend but at that moment, that felt like nothing but a title. We'd hung out a few times, usually in a group situation, and we'd been in constant phone and text contact. But that wasn't the same as actually being together, just the two of us, potentially in a face-to-face, pressing body contact kind of way…

I took a deep breath and tried to calm my nerves. It didn't work, so I decided to move onto the next stage of preparation - the outfit. That easily kept me distracted for the best part of an hour. Riley had told me to 'dress to impress' but without knowing where we were going, I couldn't work out what to wear. That dress might be perfect, or it could be over the top. And what about the shoes? Were we walking miles, or standing somewhere all night? I decided to text him to try to gain more information. This was important to us girls.

Never you mind where we're going, came the reply,

I'm sure you'll look gorgeous in whatever you wear.
They just don't get it.
I eventually opted for a pair of tight, dark jeans (always good), a black and grey striped vest (in case we were going somewhere hot, like a club), a black blazer (to smarten it up/keep me warm in case we weren't) and a pair of black strappy shoes (with a heel somewhere in the middle). I spent what seemed like forever on my hair and make-up, blow-drying it into soft bouncing curls (thank-you hair department for the tutorial) and applying a subtle mix of smokey eye make-up and nude, glossy lips. Kissing was definitely going to happen tonight, and my heart skipped an excited beat in anticipation. That, I could handle. That, I was looking forward to. But what the kissing was leading to…heart palpitation time.
I couldn't really work out why. It wasn't like I didn't know what to do. But it was our first time, and he was only my second…
Third, I corrected, the image of Lane filling my mind and making my heart do a heavy, guilty thud. My poor heart wouldn't be able to take much more of this gymnastics. I stood up from my dressing table and looked at my reflection. Without knowing where we were going or what we were doing, I had dressed to impress nonetheless.
I checked the time, which seemed to have evaporated. How had I been getting ready for the best part of three hours?! I put a clutch bag together with some essentials and headed downstairs. Seth was stretched out on the couch.
"What do you think?"
"Very nice."

"I have no idea where I'm going, it's a surprise, so I didn't know what to wear…"
Seth was watching the TV. He didn't care. It was at times like this I knew why I loved living with Steph so much. I pulled out my phone and texted her.
Hey. Missing you. Going on a date with Riley tonight - finally! Wish me luck. What you doing? x
The door buzzed and both Seth and I looked over at it.
"It's not Steph," he said, by way of confirmation. I nodded and pushed my hair behind my ears but on account of the curls, it fell back again immediately. I stared at Seth. He grinned.
"Go have fun. Enjoy yourself. Who knows when you'll see him again?"
I nodded. He was right. Whatever the night had in store, it was a damn sight better than a long distance phone-call.
"I really can make myself scarce if you want me to…" Seth called, as I reached the door. Holding the handle, I paused.
"That's okay," I called back. "He has his own apartment anyway."
I left the apartment to the sound of a wolf-whistle and cringed.
I headed downstairs and outside, praying the paparazzi/fans weren't there. I'd lucked out. The sidewalk was free of judgement. Riley's car was parked but he hadn't got out. It was no wonder why - it was *freezin*g. I crossed my arms and hurried to his car, immediately regretting not wearing a coat and having open-toe shoes.
I slid into the seat and shut the door before turning to look at him. His mere presence made my whole

body pulse with desire, a full-body heartbeat of extreme proportions. Riley seemed to fill his half of the car, which wasn't surprising given that all six feet of him was squeezed in wearing a chunky grey wool coat. A coat - how sensible.
But I was feeling anything *but* sensible. I felt myself being drawn towards him with a need to take that chiselled jaw firmly between my hands, push that casual floppy tendril of hair from his face and plant a kiss on those soft, smirking lips… In fact, I hadn't moved at all. I seemed frozen to the spot. My outside was calm, but my insides were chaos.
"Hey," he drawled in his deep, dark tone of voice and I quivered some more.
"Hey," I managed to force out, moistening my lips nervously. He watched me, his eyes staring at my mouth. I read that as a mutual desire to kiss me right back. But if he was a mess inside too, he wasn't giving anything away. He started the engine, put the car into drive and pulled away. The kisses were going to have to wait.
In fact, I realised, Riley had a bit of an agenda when it came to kisses that night. After we arrived at this trendy-looking place in Lower Manhattan and got parked, Riley led me inside and straight to the bar to order drinks. I stood beside him, *close* beside him (on account of how busy the place was), and breathed him in. A heady mix of aftershave, testosterone and pure desire made me feel light-headed. I actively clamped both my hands around my clutch to prevent myself from grabbing him by the scruff of the neck and pressing my lips on his. If he was able to control himself around me, then I didn't have much choice but to try and do the

same.
"So I have an idea," he confessed, as he led me over to a quiet corner booth. He slipped in one side, me the other, and we slid together with a bump. Sharing a grin, he put his drink down, turned his body towards me and lay his arm on the seat behind me. I had his full attention and he had mine.
"And this idea…?"
He nodded, pushing his fingers through his hair just like he did in that Dynamic Jeans commercial. *So* hot.
"Well, I thought it might be kind of fun to see how long we could go without kissing each other."
Kind of fun? More like torture, I mused. I looked at him quizzically, which he noticed, and smiled.
"Don't read too much into this. This isn't anything but a way for us to a have a little fun with each other…"
He leaned towards me and I stupidly thought he was going to kiss me, even though he'd just said he wouldn't. Instead, he pushed my hair to one side and brought his mouth to my ear.
"Before we get to the real fun, of course," he whispered in my ear, his breath on my neck fuelling a deep desire to skip the night altogether and go straight to his apartment. So apparently I wasn't feeling apprehensive anymore…
As he pulled away, I looked into his eyes. He looked right back and smiled at me. On the one hand, I was nervous, to the point of being glad we were sitting down so I didn't have to contend with this weak-at-the-knees feeling he brought out in me. But he also brought out feelings of another

kind. I somehow felt at ease with him, I trusted him. It was the perfect combination of emotions to be entering into this date - and this night - with.
I reached for my glass and held it out towards him. "To no kissing."
He took his glass and clinked it with mine, staring at me with his dark brown eyes. They were full of desire and it thrilled me to know this was a two-way thing. This challenge was going to be hard for the both of us.
"Let's dance," he said, shuffling out of the booth and holding out his hand to me. I obliged, taking off my blazer and dropping it onto the seat behind me. As I turned to take his hand, I saw him checking me out. Checking *all* of me out. Mission accomplished. I slid my hand into his and we made our way to the dance floor.
"I remember when I had to drag you to dance!" I called above the music, laying my hands on his chest. He shrugged and smiled and began to dance to the music, Ja Rule's 'Livin' It Up'. It had a good beat but we had clear intentions, whatever the song, and that was to use it to tease the hell out of each other. With every purposeful grind of my hips, with every twirl under his arm, the game was fully on. His eyes were always on me and one quick glance around the room told me I had the best-looking date in the house. Right at the end of the song, he deliberately walked into me, his arms around my back to support me as I stumbled backwards and giggled.
"You, me, bathroom, *now!*" he whispered, as he nuzzled his face into my neck. I clung to him, snug in his embrace, and grinned. He stood me back

upright and I waved my finger side to side, smiling a teasing smile.
"Nu-uh," I smirked. "I intend on making the most of you tonight."
"The feeling's mutual," he smirked right back, and I suddenly felt the need to sit down again.
Back in the booth, we made the most of the dark, cramped conditions and sat practically on top of each other. We conversed, sure, but I wasn't really listening much. I was focused on stirring my straw in my drink seductively, fluttering my eyelashes as I dropped my gaze in a bashful manner, ensuring my knee was touching his at all times. It was as though every date I'd ever had, every movie I'd ever watched, every piece of advice I'd ever been given about how to seduce a man, had been learned and stored for this very occasion.
In contrast, I was pretty sure all he had to do was just be sitting opposite me in order to make me desire him. I'd forgotten just how exceptionally handsome he was. When we talked on the phone, I had an image of him in my mind but it didn't even come close to what was sitting opposite me right now. He was an image of pure perfection.
"So," he said with a pause, just long enough for his eyes to dart across my face and settle on my lips. "How you doing over there?"
I nodded confidently.
"I'm fine."
He reached up and tugged on the neckline of his black top, indicating he was hot under the collar. I tried to hide a smile by biting my lip, which he noticed, and animatedly wiped his brow in response. I giggled.

"Shall we get out of here?" he asked.
I must have shown the panic I was feeling inside across my face because Riley let out a laugh and placed his hand on my back.
"We're not going home yet, you little minx…"
I blushed.
"I just know somewhere else we can go," he smiled.
I nodded and reached for my clutch. After keeping my cards close all night, I'd just shown him my entire hand.
He took the lead as we left the bar and I noticed we were being noticed. A few people called out our names and Riley raised his hand to acknowledge them, calm and confident and in control. He led me by the hand down the street and the excited chatter of the sidewalk crowd eventually faded out, as we paced along the cold, dark streets of the city.
"You must be cold," he said. "Here."
He reached up to unbutton his coat and I raised my hand.
"Then you'll be cold," I stated, shaking my head. "I chose this silly, girly outfit. It's only right I freeze to death in it."
Riley laughed.
"Well…" he purred, nudging his body into mine, "I appreciate the effort. It might be cold out here but you…look…*hot*."
I turned my head towards him and raised an eyebrow. He furrowed his, then shook his head, eyes closed.
"That was a horrible line," he said, and I giggled. "I'm genuinely sorry to have inflicted that on you."
I laughed a little more, then waved my hand dismissively.

"I've heard worse."
"Like what?"
"Umm… oh, yeah. So I was at this TV convention thing, during the first season of the show. And this guy walks up to me and holds out his hand and says, 'Hi. I'm Mr Right. I understand you've been looking for me…'"
Riley winced and I nodded, wide-eyed.
"I know, right?"
"What did you say?"
I pulled an awkward face.
"I think I just laughed, actually. I mean, I apologised and tried to be nice about it but I couldn't help myself!"
"Well, thank you for not laughing in my face then, I guess," Riley said, putting his hands in his pockets and kicking a stone ahead of him. He was pouting and looking sorry for himself, but I was pretty sure he was just acting.
"Aww," I said, playing along and sliding my arm into his, cuddling up to him, if not for the proximity then the warmth. We walked along like that for a while until Riley stopped and pointed.
"You been here before?" he asked, and I looked at the sign. 'Use Once & Destroy'. Twisted metal, flames coming out of the top… I'd definitely have remembered this place.
"Uh, no," I said politely. Riley wrapped his arm firmly around me and pulled me into him with a bump.
"You're gonna love it!" he enthused, but as we crossed the road and I noticed the leather-clad doorman, I wasn't so sure. He'd put us on the guest-list, which meant we walked straight in. It

also meant he'd pre-planned this part of the date, but I couldn't for the life of me figure out why. This was biker boy heaven, heavy metal blasting from the speakers and dark walls encroaching on the already cramped, sweaty space. Riley took a firm hold of me from behind, his hands on my shoulders, and steered me through the crowd. I kept bumping into people, people I'd rather not be bumping into in any capacity, although rather here than down some dark alley. I didn't mean to be judgemental - you know, each to their own. But I was clearly *not* their own. I had a pair of leather trousers, sure, but they were purely for fashion reasons.

When we reached the bar, I couldn't help but ask, "What are we doing here?"

"You'll see," Riley grinned, leaning towards me and kissing my cheek. He jerked back and stared at me.

"What?"

"I just kissed you," he said in a panic.

"That doesn't count," I said.

"It doesn't?"

"No."

He nodded to himself and I watched as a sneaky smile began at the corner of his mouth before stretching into a full-on smirk.

"So..." he said, reaching up to push my hair aside before grabbing a firm but gentle hold of the back of my neck and planting a kiss just under my earlobe. "Does that count?"

My eyes closed, I reached out to hold onto his waist to steady myself. As he pulled away, I opened my eyes and forced myself to look completely unbothered by the internal meltdown he'd just

caused inside me.
"Uh, no," I replied lightly. He flashed me a smile and I smiled back.
"What about..." he continued, and I closed my eyes, bracing myself for what was to come. He kissed me square on the nose and I squinted, my face breaking out in a grin.
"That okay?" he asked.
"Yeah, sure," I replied, and he laughed.
We caught the attention of the barman and ordered drinks. I took it as my opportunity to return the favour, so I moved around behind him and slid my hand onto his waist. I reached up with my other hand, snaking it across his chest, feeling the ripples of what lay underneath and thinking how much I wanted my hand to be underneath his top, not above it. Focussing on my play, I stretched up on tiptoes and kissed the back of his neck, pressing my body in his back and holding him tightly. I felt his hand lay itself over mine and press hard. I knew *his* eyes were closed this time. As I stood down again, he kept a hold of my hand and I felt him kiss the back of it. Three to one? I had to up my game.
I made my way under his arm and around in front of him again, stretching up to kiss his neck and then, as he looked down at me and held me in his gaze, it took all my willpower not to finish this foreplay fun by just kissing him square on the lips. Instead, I kissed his cheek then practically jumped away from him, knowing I had to enforce a little distance between us if we were to keep this charade up. Riley handed me my drink and we clinked our glasses again, toasting perhaps to our impressive display of (almost) affection.

"Come with me," he instructed, taking me by the hand and snaking us through the sweaty crowd. There was a stage ahead and I read the draped sign that hung behind the unused equipment. Eyes wide, I jumped on the spot and tugged on his hand. "Cherry Soda?!"

He turned to look at me and grinned. I reached up and threw my arm around his neck, pulling him close to me and laying one, two, three, four, five kisses in quick succession on his cheek. Screw the kiss count; he'd brought me to see my - *our* - favourite band.

We found a space big enough for us to stand, me in front of him, near to the stage. We didn't get bothered because, to be honest, I don't think anyone there was a big fan of teen TV shows. Riley distracted me by kissing my neck and running his hands up and down my sides until the band came out on stage.

They played an amazing set. It was incredible to be so close to them…and so close to Riley. Mostly we stood like that, with his arms around me, but sometimes I turned to face him and sang to him, or he'd lean his head forwards and I'd turn my head so I could see him. Every line we sang to each other cemented our mutual love for the band and, arguably, for each other. This was what dating someone was all about. The shared experiences. The close proximity. And the secret desire for your favourite band in the world to just hurry up the hell up and finish the set so we could *really* get on with the night….

As we left the bar, I excitedly tugged on his hand, pulling him close to me.

"I can't believe we just did that! I love them so much."
He nodded and smiled.
"Me too."
"Just another thing we have in common…" I mused aloud, walking along beside him. He began to slow and I did too, until we came to a stop. He looked at me and I looked at him, our bodies turned towards each other. He stepped forwards, the already close space between us closing even smaller. I tipped my head to look up at him, into his brown, brooding eyes.
I sensed it before it even happened. I didn't gloat in the win, I just savoured his loss, as he pressed his lips against mine and finally kissed me. It didn't matter that we were standing in the middle of the street. That kiss had been six weeks, two days and twenty-three hours coming. There was no stopping us. I reached up to hold his face in my hands as he wrapped his warm arms around me and pulled me into him.
When he stopped, I was disappointed. He reached his hand up to lay it gently against my cold cheek.
"I think it's time we added something else to that list of things we have in common."
Now *that* was a line.
Back in the car, I checked my phone. Steph had replied.
Hey sweetie. Sorry I missed you. I'll explain all later. So much to tell you… Hope you're having fun with Riley x
I wondered just how much could possibly have happened at her photo shoot, but I had much more pressing things on my mind. Like exactly how much fun Riley and I were about to have together.

My heart fluttered with anticipation.
The drive felt like forever, even though it was barely fifteen minutes. We walked to his apartment and rode the elevator awkwardly. I dared a glance in his direction. Surely Mr Confidence wasn't feeling *nervous*...
He fumbled his keys letting us into the apartment. Oh my God, he was. That made him all the more charming and desirable, and I very nearly kicked the door open myself just to get things going.
Finally, we went inside. I looked around. The last time I'd been here it had been full of people, on account of it being his birthday party. But now it was just the two of us, and it seemed huge.
"Can I get you something to drink?" Riley asked, breezing past me and heading into the kitchen. I followed, my eyes drawn to the corner, where I'd given him that awkward version of a lap-dance. I cringed and followed my gaze back to him, where he was waiting beside the refrigerator.
"Oh, uh, just a glass of water will be fine."
He got a glass and filled it up and handed it to me. I caught his eye with mine and he looked away. His nerves were making me nervous, and I simply couldn't take much more of that, so I took a quick sip then placed the glass down on the side. I reached for his hand and took it, drawing his attention back to me. I looked up, he looked down, and we came together for a kiss.
As the kiss began to turn more passionate, and he pressed me against the counter with clear intentions, my nerves began to melt away, replaced with clear intentions of my own. But surely we weren't going to do it here, in the kitchen?

I stopped and pulled away, catching my breath.
"Are you okay?" he asked, his eyes full of concern. I nodded, stroking his cheek.
"I was just wondering if we could, uh, maybe move this somewhere else…"
He smirked.
"What, my granite counter top isn't doing it for you?"
I screwed up my nose and shook my head with a smile. He nodded and took my hand, leading me out of the kitchen and down the hall. I knew where his bedroom was, so it surprised me when he led me to the left, not the right. He took me towards a glass door and opened it. It led to the balcony.
I tugged on his hand and he looked at me.
"You're kidding me, right?"
"What?"
I arched an eyebrow at him and he rolled his eyes with a smile. He disappeared outside and I stood there. If he thought I was going to…*outside*…well, he had another thing coming. But when he reappeared, it was with a huge, thick, faux fur blanket and a come-to-bed smile. He wrapped it around me and pulled me closer to him, kissing me and making me realise we could definitely generate a decent amount of heat between us, even without the blanket.
He led me outside walking backwards, unable to stop kissing me, and over to an outdoor day-bed kind of thing. The blanket wrapped around us both, we half fell onto it, a tangle of arms and legs and kisses that had begun to go beyond our control. The wheels were off and we were full-steam ahead. Yanking off our clothes in a series of

twisted, difficult contortions, we finally found ourselves face-to-face, in a pressing body contact kind of way.

I took a moment to look into his eyes. But it was only a brief moment, because I had nothing to question. I wanted him, I wanted this, and the time was now.

I was pretty sure his reputation wasn't as wild or extensive as the press claimed it was. But whatever the truth was behind that, he certainly lived up to the reputation I had built up in my mind. It was new and different and everything I could have hoped for, and *then* some. As he held me in his arms, wrapping the blanket tight around our hot, sweaty bodies, I felt cherished. And I definitely hadn't expected that.

On account of the romance of the situation giving out to the reality (that we were both too tall for the blanket and our feet were turning numb with cold), we shuffled inside together and into the warmth and comfort of his bed for Round Two. And Three. Well, it had been a long time coming…

FEBRUARY 15TH

I left Riley's the morning after with a definite spring in my step. I was sad that we weren't going to see each other again for who knows how long, but my cravings had been satisfied - very, *very* satisfied - and I'd even been given one final treat, as I'd kissed him goodbye at his door.
He'd stroked my cheek tenderly and gazed into my eyes.
"You really are something special, you know that?"
I beamed and gazed lovingly right back. He took a deep breath and looked at me sincerely.
"I'm really falling for you," he confessed, and I had only a moment to ensure I responded in the right way. But what was the right way? I went with my gut.
"The feeling's mutual," I said with a smile, closing my eyes and kissing him again.
So it wasn't exactly 'I love you' but it was a strong

step in the right direction. As I let myself into my apartment, I was fit to burst. I sure hoped someone was home that I could talk to.
I knew right away they were. I could hear voices in the distant, upstairs somewhere. I closed the door behind me and threw my clutch on the floor, kicking off my shoes and hurrying ahead with excitement. But as I got further into the apartment, I tuned into the noise. That wasn't conversation; that was an argument. I began to slow my pace until I reached the bottom of the stairs.
"What are you talking about?!"
Seth.
"I can't…I can't talk to you right now."
Steph.
Uh oh. I looked around the apartment. I really didn't need to be here right now. But before I could grab my stuff and sneak back out, the door to their bedroom flew open and Steph came out. Her blond hair was messy and she looked harassed. I stood frozen to the spot.
"Beccy."
"I just…I came back and…I'm gonna go," I thumbed at the door, and she wide-eyed me.
"No, don't," she stressed urgently, descending the stairs in a hurry. Seth emerged from the bedroom and watched as she reached the bottom and flung her arms around me.
"Help me," she hushed at me, and I held onto her. Help her with what? Seth pointed down the stairs at us.
"You need to talk some sense into her. She's acting crazy."
He came down the stairs next, and Steph stood

beside me. I felt like I was between two giant forces of energy.
"She's leaving!" Seth said, jabbing a finger in Steph's direction. This was news to me.
"What?" I asked.
Steph looked at Seth, then at me, lowering her gaze sheepishly.
"I just…I can't be here right now."
She looked at me, pleading with her eyes.
"Help me, Beccy, please."
I didn't know what she was doing, or what she talking about, so how could I possibly help her? I looked at Seth, who appeared just as confused as me but also with an added layer of hurt and rejection. I reached out and put my hand on Steph's shoulder just as the front door swung open.
"Okay guys, they were all out of bagels so I got us some French toast inste-"
Josh trailed off upon apparently entering a crisis zone. Holding three cups of coffee in a cardboard carrier, with a paper bag tucked under his arm, he stopped in his tracks as all three of us stared at him. The door clicked shut behind him.
"What's going on?"
"Steph's packing up her stuff and leaving and she won't say why," Seth explained, and I took the opportunity to catch Steph's eye and glare at her, silently asking her what the hell was going on. She shook her head, clearly worried, which in turn made *me* worried. Josh put the stuff down on the kitchen counter and walked apprehensively towards us, his hands raised in defence.
"O-*kay*," he said slowly. "Maybe we can all just…"
"Josh, I don't want to talk," Steph cut him off. "I

just…I want to leave."
She started off up the stairs at a run and Seth looked at both of us before hurrying after her. Josh came towards me and put his hand on my shoulder.
"You take her, I'll take him," he instructed and I nodded, the two of us rushing up the stairs behind them. Steph was grabbing clothes from her wardrobe and throwing them onto the bed, as Seth tried to block her, holding her by the arms and trying to look into her eyes. But she was looking everywhere but back at him and I knew what that meant. She didn't just want out of the apartment - she wanted out of their relationship.
"Seth, buddy, let's just give Steph some space," Josh said calmly, reaching between them and taking Seth by the shoulder.
"She's leaving!" he snapped at Josh, and Josh nodded.
"If that's the case, then you can't stop her."
"What?"
"Steph?" Josh said, and she looked at him.
"He deserves an explanation. You know that."
She looked with shame down at her feet.
"So if we give you some space, will you promise me you won't leave without explaining why?"
She paused, then nodded her head. Seth stepped back, Josh let him go, then they both made their way out of the room. Josh gave me a supportive pat on the shoulder as he passed by, like a tag team. If only I knew what *I* was meant to do. Josh shut the door and Steph and I were alone. She raised her eyes to look at me and I hurried towards her as she came towards me, both of us wrapping our arms

around each other.
"Oh, Beccy."
"Steph, what the hell's going on?" I asked gently, stroking her hair. She held me tightly and I held her back, then she stepped away and looked at me. Guilt was etched across her face.
"It's Freddie."
"What's Freddie?" I asked stupidly.
"He's the reason I'm leaving."
My mind tried to play catch up but I couldn't make sense of the situation. Freddie? As in, our brothers' friend Freddie King? What did he have to do with anything? And then…boom. It hit me. Although it filled me with an uneasy, uncertain feeling of strangeness, I knew what was going on.
My furrowed brow must have said it all because she nodded in confirmation.
"Freddie?" I asked aloud, and she stared at the door behind me. Maybe I'd said it too loud, as she reached for my hand and led me to the bed, and we sat down, perched on top of her pile of clothes.
"Yes, Freddie."
"But when did this happen?"
"After New Year's Eve."
My mind raced back to that night, playing it through in a series of stills. He'd arrived. They'd hugged. He was in the VIP area. She'd been watching him. But Jenna had been there, trying her luck.
"But I thought…" I began, and she shook her head.
"He wasn't interested in Jenna," she explained.
"Turns out he was, well, he was interested in *me*."
"But you…"
She nodded and shrugged.

"I know," she said solemnly, before a hint of a smile began to form. "But I just…I can't help it, Beccy. I can't help how I feel about him."
I raised both my hands at her and shook my head. This was too much. Information overload.
"Wait a minute, this is Freddie we're talking about. Goofy oddball Freddie, who used to hang out with us when we were kids."
"We were in middle school when he moved to town," Steph noted, raising a pointed finger. "And you've got to admit, he's one of the good guys."
"That goes without saying but so is…"
Seth. My silence somehow said his name aloud. Steph dropped her gaze and began twiddling her fingers.
"I don't know what to say to him."
"Steph, you're going to have to catch me up because are you saying… you're leaving Seth?" I asked.
She nodded. I sat back, shaking my head in disbelief.
"How can you possibly…I mean, how long has this been going on?"
"We went on a date last week…"
"Steph!"
She looked at me.
"What the *hell*?" I said, lowering my voice. "Why didn't you tell me?"
"I couldn't. I couldn't tell anyone," she said, shaking her head.
"But I'm your best friend."
"Which is why you're still the first person I'm telling," she said, reaching out to lay her hands on my knees. "Albeit a little late."

I sighed.
"Steph, I'm shocked. I really am."
"I know. So am I. I never expected to have such strong feelings for someone, especially not so quickly."
"So where are you going?" I asked, trying to piece together this very confusing puzzle.
"To his," she said simply. I wide-eyed her.
"Are you kidding me?"
"No."
"Steph! You can't just move in with him!"
"Why not?" she shrugged.
"Because…you've been together for what, a week?"
She nodded, then rolled her eyes.
"I know this seems crazy but…"
"Steph, this *is* crazy."
She looked at me with strong determination behind her tear-stained eyes.
"I know how I feel about him. And I know how he feels about me. This is happening, whether you, or Seth, or anyone likes it."
"Steph," I said calmly, reaching out to touch her arm. "You know I'll always be behind you, no matter what you do. It's just…well, this is stretching things a little bit."
She nodded, gently smiling.
"I know. But Beccy…"
She raised her eyes to me, full of hope and excitement and well, happiness.
"I can't tell you how much I've fallen for him."
I nodded and smiled a little back.
"Then I guess I'm happy for you."
We hugged again.
"But we still have Seth to sort out."

She held her hands to her face, blocking out the world.
"I can't…I just…I don't think I can tell him the truth."
"You have to," I stressed. "He deserves that much."
"He doesn't deserve any of this."
She wasn't wrong there. I helped her pack up the rest of her stuff (not all of it, of course, just the essentials) and we lugged two bags together to the bedroom door.
"Beccy, I don't think I can do this."
"You have to."
"I mean it. If my legs take me off running in the direction of the door, you'd better stop me."
I nodded.
"I will."
She took a deep breath and sighed it out.
"I have to do this," she said to herself. "For him."
"For Seth," I said quietly. Steph looked at me.
"No," she replied. "For Freddie."
I watched her in complete disbelief as she opened the door and stepped through it. What the hell had happened to her this week? How had quiet, mild-mannered, nice guy Freddie been the catalyst for such an epic turn of events?
We stood at the top of the stairs side by side and looked down. Josh and Seth, who'd been sitting on the couch, stood and looked up at us. *I* wanted to run for the door, so God only knows how Steph was feeling. I looked at her and she looked at me. I gave her a supportive nod and we set off down the stairs together. We put both the bags down and looked at the boys. They looked right back.
"So?" Seth said, unable to stop himself, his arms out

wide.
"I'm leaving."
"That much is clear," he said, his voice full of stress. "But why?"
Steph took a deep breath and my heart stopped. The whole room seemed to stop.
"I'm moving in with someone else."
Not *exactly* how I'd have worded it, but hey. It was out there now. Seth's face dropped. So did Josh's, and we exchanged a private glance. Forever seemed to pass until Seth asked the obvious.
"Who?"
"Freddie."
"Freddie King?"
Steph nodded. Now the boys just looked plain confused. Huh, I mused, that's how I must have looked.
"*Freddie King*?!" Seth repeated.
"Steph, what the hell…" Josh said, almost involuntarily.
"How long has this been going on?" Seth asked, coming round the couch towards her.
"Not long."
"How long?"
"Not long," she repeated, and he stared at her in exasperation.
"HOW LONG?!" he yelled, and I winced.
"A week," Steph said quietly. Josh pulled a face at me and Seth leaned his head back.
"A *week*?" he scoffed, letting out a twisted sort of laugh.
Steph sighed and put her hand on her hip, just staring at him. Seth looked back at her, the laughter fading.

"You're moving in with him after a week?" he taunted. She nodded firmly. He watched her, confusion spreading across his face. It didn't make sense, but it was the reality of the situation, and it still meant she was leaving.
"I don't understand," he said.
"No one can. This is between Freddie and I."
I looked at Steph. Josh looked at Steph. Seth's eyes nearly popped out of his head. He slammed his hand onto his chest.
"What about me?!"
Steph sighed, closing her eyes.
"I didn't mean it like that… I just meant…"
"You know what? Go," Seth said, waving his hand dismissively at her. Steph looked at him as he shook his head in confusion.
"You're not you right now. I don't know you right now. So just go."
Steph didn't need to be told twice. She picked up her bag and I grabbed the other one, carrying it to the door. We'd only just got there when Seth came running across the apartment.
"No, Steph, I'm sorry. I didn't mean that. Don't go," he said, grabbing hold of her and wrapping his arms around her. She stood sadly and let him, but she didn't respond. I stepped back and found myself beside Josh, who put his arm around me supportively. This was heart-breaking, for all involved.
"Seth, I'm sorry."
"Steph," Seth pleaded, holding her face in her hands. "Don't do this. Please."
She closed her eyes, shutting him out.
"I'm already gone," she replied sadly. There was a

horrible moment of realisation, of everything coming to a head. Seth stepped back, keeping his hand on her cheek until the very last moment. She grabbed both bags and shuffled through the door, looking back not at him but at me, one last time. Her eyes full of tears, I felt completely connected to her in that moment. I understood her completely. Because I'd been in that very situation last year. It was a choice, of sorts, but the decision had already been made, somewhere deep inside her. She loved someone else now.

The feel of Josh's arm around me made me feel guilty all over again. But as the door shut, and Seth turned to face us, his eyes wide with disbelief and complete and utter sadness, I put my own emotions on hold as we both rushed forwards towards him.

***

It was a horrible afternoon. Seth was in pieces and to top it off, Steph was calling me and asking me to come round to Freddie's. I felt so torn. Of course my loyalties lay with my best friend but I cared for Seth too, and he was the very unlucky, very unwilling victim in all this.

"Go," Josh said to me, taking me aside in the kitchen.

"Are you sure?"

"She needs you," he said, and I nodded.

"Oh God, this is just awful."

"Break-ups always are."

I looked up at him and he pulled me towards him, giving me a hug and a kiss on the head.

"We're cool," he said by way of confirmation, and I nodded, feeling a little better.
"So I guess I'll see you later?" I said.
He nodded and rolled his eyes, running his fingers through his hair as he returned to the living room to deal with Seth. I slipped on my Converses, realising I still hadn't got changed out of my date clothes, but I knew I had more pressing issues than wearing an outfit twice. I did, however, grab my coat this time.

***

Steph had explained that although Freddie lived in Philadelphia still, he'd been staying in a hotel near Battery Park for the past week so they could spend more time together. So it was the hotel that I hitched a cab to, and I found myself tentatively knocking at the door of Room 313. As if that wasn't an omen...
Steph opened the door and smiled with relief when she saw me. We hugged and I looked around. It was a suite, so it had a separate sleeping and living area, but it was small and I saw Freddie right away. He got up from the chair and came wandering over.
"Hey Beccy."
"Hey Freddie."
Oh God, this was even more awkward than I'd imagined it would be. I'd known Freddie for the best part of six years and we had what I'd have called a pretty close, easygoing kind of relationship. He may have been my older brother David's friend first, but over the years, after many

house-calls, parties and Thanksgivings, he'd become my friend too. But right now, I felt like I didn't know him at all. Or Steph, for that matter.
"I'm just going to use the bathroom. Sorry, excuse me," Steph said, and with that, we were alone. I looked at Freddie, who stood with his hands in the pockets of his jeans, his shoulders hunched apologetically.
"Look, I know this is out of the blue..."
"Out of the blue?" I returned, wide-eyeing him. "Freddie, this is insane."
He came towards me.
"Look, you know me, okay?"
Barely, I mused.
"You know I would never do this if I wasn't serious about her. I really care about her."
I pushed my fingers through the tangle of curls that was last night's hairdo. I removed my hand almost immediately.
"I'm just trying to play catch-up here. What changed?"
He shrugged.
"I don't know."
"How long have you...had feelings for her?" I asked, the words tumbling awkwardly from my mouth.
"This hasn't been some yearning secret crush, if that's what you mean. But when I saw her at New Year, something changed inside me. I felt...differently about her."
Steph emerged from the bathroom and looked between us. It was obvious we were talking about her.
"I was just asking Freddie about what's going on," I

explained anyway.
Steph nodded and went to stand beside him. He put his arm around her shoulder and she cuddled up beside him, wrapping her arms around his middle. I simply watched them. They both looked at me then stepped apart. They had this natural chemistry already, a comfortable ease around each other, but it was still strange to me.
"I know this must be weird for you," Steph said.
"Honestly? I can't get my head around it."
"Neither can we really," Freddie said, as Steph gazed up at him. Okay, this was too much. I walked past them and went to sit on a chair. They sat beside each other on a formal-looking couch.
"What do you want to know?" Steph asked.
I let out a sigh and sat back in my chair.
"I don't know, guys. I…"
"Like I said, we went for a date last week and…" Steph began to explain.
"But how did things go from New Year's Eve to date?" I asked, gesticulating with my hands.
"Freddie texted me. We just sort of texted back and forth for a bit, didn't we?"
He nodded.
"I wanted to see more of her, but I knew she was with Seth," Freddie said, looking sheepishly at me.
"But that didn't stop you?"
He shook his head.
"Beccy, you know this isn't like me. Or Freddie," Steph said, "We'd never set out to hurt anyone. But once we'd started talking, I just…I knew I had to explore my feelings. I was curious as to why I was feeling this way about him."
"And once we went on that date, it was obvious."

I nodded, watching them share a sweet, smitten glance at each other. Although I couldn't quite believe it, I could see it with my very own eyes - there was definitely something real and genuine going on between them.
We sat for a while and talked, mostly about everything *but* them. It was actually quite nice, once I got past the weirdness at knowing they were together now. Freddie had to take a phone call, which left Steph and I alone. I went and sat beside her.
"Beccy, you're on board with this, right?" she asked, turning towards me and taking my hands in hers.
"Do I have much choice?" I smiled. She remained serious.
"Because everyone's going to hate me. *Everyone*."
"No, they won't."
She sighed.
"Do you know that feeling, when everything inside your head is screaming to make a different choice but you just know, with your whole heart and soul, that you won't? That you can't? That you're going to do the one thing that's going to hurt someone?"
I nodded.
"Of course I do. I did the same thing with Riley. To Josh."
Steph nodded, her eyes wide with hope.
"Maybe he'll be okay, you know? Maybe Seth can forgive me, like Josh did with you."
I nodded.
"Absolutely. Who knows? But these things take time. And sweetie, this was a big shock for him. For all of us."
Steph nodded.

"I know. And I'm going to have to be patient and live with my decision."
I nodded back and she raised her eyes, holding me in a firm stare.
"But you know what? I really think I've made the right one."
I had no idea if she was right. But as I left the two of them later that night, and saw the way they casually came together to embrace each other, side by side, to wave me off, I wondered if she might be right.
Hell, I'd been right about Riley. When the world was telling me to steer clear, not to fall for the bad boy, he'd only break my heart, I'd listened to my instincts and gone for it. And he'd turned out to be just wonderful. He'd exceeded my expectations, not disappointed them.
Back at the apartment, I slumped down on the sofa beside Josh and realised the full extent at how perfect my situation had turned out to be. Loving boyfriend, loving *ex*-boyfriend. *Perfect.*
"How is he?" I asked, as Josh glanced up the stairs towards Steph and Seth's room. He rubbed his eyes and yawned.
"As expected. He's completely devastated. How's Steph?"
"Kind of…resolute, actually. She's sure she's done the right thing, even if she went about it in the wrong way."
Josh rubbed under his chin with the fingers of his hand and stared at me.
"Is that how you felt?"
"No. I wasn't at all sure after we broke up. I didn't hear from Riley for a long time, and besides, we

weren't together then. Nothing had happened at that point."
Josh nodded.
"Do you think they'll ever get to the same place that we have?" I mused aloud.
Josh paused thoughtfully.
"Perhaps."
I nodded and gazed at the side of his face, his attention returned to the TV.
"You know, we only have what we have now because of you," I noted.
"Uh, I think you'll find…"
"No, I mean, okay, so it was *me* that broke us up," I agreed, looking at him with gentle, smiling eyes.
He turned his head to look at me.
"But it was *you* that kept us together," I concluded.
He smiled softly at me before lifting his arm up and laying it around my shoulders. I snuggled into him and we both watched the TV together until I could no longer keep my eyes open.
"Time to hit the sack," I concluded with a yawn and a stretch. Josh reached for the blanket folded up on the arm of the sofa and nodded in agreement.
"You know, I'll confess," I said, "tonight of all night's, I'm glad this is the apartment where I get to keep the bed."
"Yeah, yeah, Beccy, don't rub it in," Josh said, giving me a playful shove as I stood up from the sofa. I watched as he moved to stretch out, patting the cushion before laying his head on it. I got the bed here, he got the bed in Lexington. It had seemed the only fair thing to do at the time. We'd agreed it was only going to be a temporary thing

because I think we'd both assumed it would become unbearable – not just the sleeping arrangements, but living together overall. But here we were, months later, and nothing had changed. I wasn't entirely sure that Steph and Seth would be able to salvage that kind of closeness but I certainly wished it for them.

FEBRUARY 18th

It was that time of the year again - awards season. Having not even started filming for my first movie yet, receiving any accolades of my own was still a distant dream. But the Stars and Hype Awards were always good to the show, and we weren't surprised to be up for the 'Coolest Cast' award again.

I excitedly called Riley to find out if he was going, visions of the two of us making our first public appearance together consuming all my spare thoughts. I was beyond crushed to find out that yes, Hazy Days was nominated but no, he wasn't going. 'Conflict with the schedule', he explained, noting that Lori and Selena were going instead, without the boys.

I was moaning to Meghan about it later in her trailer when Karl, our show runner, popped in. "Hey, you two," he said, closing the door behind

him. "I was just wondering if you girls had made any decisions on going to the Stars and Hype Awards yet."
Meghan and I exchanged a glance.
"Is it even a choice?" I asked.
Karl nodded.
"Of course. You know, it does cost the network a lot of money to send all you guys out to LA First Class."
I nodded understandingly. I was already taking the showbiz perks for granted - my Mom would have scolded me if she'd been there.
"Thing is," Karl said, "they want you *all* to go. It's a week before the explosion episode and they really want you guys to be seen, to push the show to the biggest audience possible."
Meghan and I both nodded, first at each other, then at Karl.
"I mean, sure. It's hardly like work, is it?" Meghan said.
"Oh, Beccy, that reminds me," Karl said. "Who's your date?"
I slumped into my seat.
"I was hoping to go with Riley but he's working so…"
"Perfect!" Karl said, happily clapping his hands together. I frowned at him.
"Sorry, sweetheart, I didn't mean it like that. It's just we were hoping you would go with Josh."
"With Josh?" I asked incredulously. "But why?"
"Well, I doubt it's escaped your knowledge but your break-up wasn't exactly well received by the fans. In fact, there's been a drop in ratings, which we can't *directly* attribute to you guys, *but…*"

I stared at Karl in disbelief. Our break-up was affecting the show? But how? Casey and Jonny were still together. And Josh and I had managed to put all our issues aside to be professional and work together. I wondered why I really hadn't known about all the negative reaction to our split. I actively avoided reading the tabloids (something my parents had advised me very early on in my career) but things like that were up to Trish to tell me. I understood now - Trish would have felt horrible telling me that, when she knew how hard the split had been and how good things were finally going between us. Maybe she'd made a professional decision, but my gut told me it had been a personal one.
"Anyway," Karl said, "if you both go to the awards, you know, and show everyone how great you guys are together still, then we really think that would help boost the ratings again."
I nodded slowly, unable to fully absorb what was being asked of me. It was so...controlling. I was totally being bribed, except with no apparent pay-off for me. Karl gave us a wave and disappeared, and Meghan was by my side in a shot.
"Oh my God, Beccy, what the hell?"
"I know, right? I mean, I'm not just making a big deal out of this, am I?"
"No way," she said, her eyes wide. "They want you to pretend to be in love with Josh still?"
"No," I replied, "that's not what they said. We just have to..."
She arched an eyebrow.
"Show everyone how great you guys are together," she quoted, and I frowned.

"Riley's going to go crazy."
Meghan sighed.
"Oh my God, yes. I hadn't even thought about him..."
I sat up and took a deep breath, pushing my hair behind my ears.
"Right, let's think about this. So Josh would have been going to the awards anyway, so it's not like we're actually going as dates. We'll all be going together. And Riley was *never* going, so it's not like I'm rejecting him, or choosing Josh over him. And besides, the network is telling me to do this. I can hardly say no, can I?"
That was essentially how I told Riley. In a text, not a phone call - I chickened out.
Well I can't say I'm very happy, came his almost immediate reply, *but if that's what you feel you have to do, then I guess you're going to go ahead and do it anyway.*
I don't have a choice, I'd replied.
You always have a choice, came the final reply, and I didn't hear from him again until after the awards show, four days later.
The awards show itself went without a hitch. Josh and I did a few interviews together, posed for a few photos, but it didn't feel uncomfortable, even when we answered questions about us.
"It just works," Josh had said to one reporter. "We used the chemistry we had as a couple and we just put it all into Casey and Jonny."
"But what about rumours that you still live together?"
"We do, yes," Josh had continued, as I gratefully looked on. "But we're friends now, and friends do

have a habit of sharing apartments, right?"
After all the drama, we didn't even win! After Steph and Seth's break-up, Seth had decided not to attend, so it was up to Steph, Nic, Alicia and Harlen to collect the 'Coolest Cast' award for Vampire High for the second time in a row. At the after-party, Steph and I finally had a quick chance to catch up.
"So how are things going with Freddie?" I asked.
"Good," she smiled. "We're living in his apartment in Philly at the moment, *but...*"
"What?"
"We're kind of thinking of moving out to LA," she said carefully, searching my face for a reaction. What she got was an explosive one.
"What?!"
"I know, I know. But Freddie has this new movie filming over there soon, and the network have been considering moving location to shoot Vampire High over there for a while now. In fact, it was Seth and I that kept them here..."
She looked at me and tentatively asked,
"How is he?"
I simply shook my head in response. She nodded in understanding.
"Okay, well...how's things with you anyway?" she asked, changing the subject.
I looked across the room towards Josh, who was chatting to Lori.
"Riley's mad at me for coming here with Josh."
"You came with Josh?"
"Not exactly..." I said, before explaining what had been asked of me.
"So you guys haven't like, flirted for the cameras?"

"Oh God, no!" I said, shaking my head. "It's all been purely platonic. Like it always is."
Steph glanced at Josh, then back at me. I read her face - she was thinking something.
"What?" I asked.
"Nothing," she said quietly. "And besides, Riley can't stay mad at you forever. You're his girlfriend."
I sure as hell hoped that status was still secure.
I also got a chance to speak to Jenna, albeit with Steph firmly on the other side of the room. They hadn't gone public with their relationship yet, but I somehow figured Jenna would have found out somehow - the Hollywood grapevine can be a very tangled one.
"So…is it true?" she asked me, cornering me with a drink in one hand and the other on her hip.
"Is what true?" I asked innocently, hoping she was referring to something else altogether.
"Steph and Freddie."
I nodded. She rolled her eyes.
"Oh, you're kidding me? I mean, come *on*…"
I didn't know what to say. I was hardly thrilled by the situation, especially not now Steph was eloping across the country with him, but I wasn't about to stab her in the back and have a bitchfest with Jenna either.
"Have you seen them together?" she asked.
I nodded.
"And?"
"It seems pretty genuine," I shrugged. Jenna sighed.
"Whatever," she said, staring into her drink before knocking it back and giving me a shrug. "You can't win 'em all."
"Don't even worry about that," I said, patting her

arm. "Take a look around - it's hot guy central in here tonight."
Jenna's eyes flashed widely as a smile returned to her face.
"I know. Did you see Harlen? He's looking positively edible."
"Yeah, but Steph did say he's got a bit of an eye for the ladies..."
I don't know if it was the mention of Steph, or the challenge of it all, but Jenna suddenly looked all fired up.
"Well, then, I'd best go put myself in his eye-line. Wish me luck."
I looked her up and down, her impeccable figure and ample cleavage squeezed into a sequinned mini-dress.
"You really don't need any," I said with a smile.
"Oh, by the way," she said, quickly spinning back round, "I'm moving to New York at the end of the month."
"Seriously?!" I replied excitedly. So one friend was moving away, but another was moving in? Life had a funny way of balancing itself out.
"I'll give you a call about the housewarming!" she called over her shoulder, as she sashayed across the room with new-found confidence.
I got so caught up in a Davey's Crowd whirlwind that it wasn't until we'd flown back to Manhattan and I'd let myself into the apartment that I thought about Riley again. Even with taking care of Seth - lending an ear, downplaying any details Steph might have given me at the party (especially about moving) and giving him a supportive hug - my mind was now firmly back on how to fix the

situation with my suspicious, jealous boyfriend.
It didn't help my case when all the magazines decided to print photographs of Josh and I the next day, with headlines like 'DAVEY'S CROWD COUPLE REUNITED ON THE RED CARPET' and 'JOSH AND BECCY TOGETHER - BUT WHERE'S RILEY?'
I kept in contact with Riley, even though it was one-sided for a while, until finally, he replied to one of my late night texts with one of his own.
I miss you, it simply said.
I miss you too. I really want to see you again.
Are you sure you're allowed *to be seen with me?* came the sarcastic response. I wished I had my team of writers on hand to respond to *that* one. This wasn't going to be easy. I wanted to talk about things face-to-face - I was pretty sure that would sort things out. But as I flicked through the schedule and knew deep in my heart his would be just as busy, I wondered exactly when I really *would* get to see him again.

MARCH 19th

Thankfully, it wasn't that long before I saw Riley again. He just turned up at the apartment one morning with a big bunch of flowers and surprised me.
Seth was staying at his parent's in Philly - he'd taken the split from Steph hard. Really hard. And no matter how many hours Josh spent effectively babysitting him, playing computer games and watching action movies and getting through what appeared to be a truckload of beer, Seth was lost. So he went home. I figured it was as good a place as any - being in the apartment he'd shared with her, sleeping in the same bed, can't have helped the situation. That only highlighted how unique things had been for Josh and I.
Thankfully for Riley and I (and I suppose Josh too), he was off filming Davey's Crowd in Lexington. So after the welcome hugs and kisses, and the show

around the apartment, it wasn't long before Riley and I were making out on my bed. And one thing led to another…
It felt so good to have him back. It had been a tense couple of weeks, what with the stupid Stars and Hype Awards stuff, and not seeing him and being able to show him how I really felt had been hard. But as soon as we were together, it was obvious the chemistry was still there.
We ordered take-out for lunch and ate it cuddled up together in our underwear. He asked me about Davey's Crowd and what was going on with Steph but frankly, I wasn't in the mood for conversation. I practically pinned him to the bed and got back to work.
It was dusk when we finally got dressed again.
"You're insatiable, you know that, woman?" he remarked, as I cuddled up behind him and watched him rifling through the refrigerator.
"Well, you are all naked in my apartment and stuff," I replied. "How do you expect me to respond?"
I snaked my hands up and across his chest and pressed myself against him, laying kisses all over the curve of his back. Riley stepped back and closed the door, and it knocked me off balance, so I stepped back too, letting him go. He took the carton of juice and held it up.
"Glass?" he asked, and I pointed to the cupboard, rocking from foot to foot. He poured himself one, offered another to me (which I declined) then stood and took a long gulp of juice. I watched him.
"What?"
"Nothing," I said, arching an eyebrow as I leaned

against the refrigerator door. "Aren't I allowed to just look at you?"
"I'm not an oil painting," he said sarcastically, taking another sip of his drink.
"I'd be inclined to disagree with you on that."
He sighed and looked at me. I nibbled on my finger and gave him a teasing, seductive look. His defences dropped and he couldn't help but smirk.
"What am I going to do with you?"
"Whatever you like."
He stalked towards me and lifted me clean off the floor, wrapping his arms around me and carrying me giggling back towards the stairs.
As darkness fell, I had to make a decision. Should I let Riley stay over knowing Josh was on his way back? Thankfully, it was one I didn't have to make as Riley decided he wanted to spend the night as his own place.
"You know, it'll be good to have at least one night there. Check it out, make sure everything's okay," he reasoned.
"Would you like some company?" I asked, cuddling up to him. He smiled down at me and kissed me on the nose.
"Thanks, babe, but my flight's real early in the morning, so…"
I felt a little rejected, but then I remember we had been at it pretty much all day, and he was probably as tired as I was. I yawned as I showed him to the door and by the time we were standing in the hallway, I was ready to starfish in my big ol' bed alone.
"So…" I said.
"So," he replied.

"Can we do this again?" I smiled seductively, stepping closer to him and looping my arms around his neck. "Preferably sometime soon."
He nodded, looking down at me before giving me a short but sweet kiss.
"I promise I'll check the schedule as soon as I get it."
I nodded. Not exactly a firm commitment but I knew the reality of our situation - the way things were going, Christmas would be the next holiday we got to celebrate together. I waved him goodbye and watched him leave, my handsome, hot hunk of a boyfriend. I grinned to myself as I shut the door behind me.

***

As I was brushing my teeth before bed, my phone rang. It was Trish.
"Sorry to bother you so late, but I thought you'd want to know. They've finally confirmed the start date for Irresponsible Actions."
I rolled my eyes as I spat out my toothpaste into the sink.
"Sorry," I apologised, "but thank God! So the prima donna finally found a window in his oh-so-busy schedule, did he?"
My upcoming co-star Oliver Rose had enjoyed a somewhat meteoric rise to fame. Securing the lead in the Teen Crusader movie, and sequel, and *third* movie, had kept him top of the box office for the last three summers and apparently, as well as inflating his bank balance, that had inflated his ego too. We'd both been cast in the movie as couple Jessica Albright and Cody Smith way back in May

last year, and the shoot had already been postponed to accommodate him. I wanted to be professional and open-minded but I was already pretty sure he was going to be a real piece of work to be around.

"So…?"

"It's April 10th. I've spoken to Paul and the other exec's and they're going to look into writing Casey out of Davey's Crowd for the duration of the shoot."

"How are they going to do that?" I pondered, heading into the bedroom and switching off the bathroom light.

"It's up to the writers to figure that out. Don't you worry," Trish said, in that soothing, in-control-of-the-situation way she had.

"Hey Trish," I said. "Why didn't you tell me that there'd been negative press about me and Josh splitting up?"

There was a pause.

"Honestly?" she said, before sighing. "I should have said something. But you guys were getting on so great, and things were picking up with Riley, and…"

"It's fine," I smiled, climbing into bed and pulling the duvet up. "I figured as much."

"Trust me when I say, I always have your best interests at heart. If there really had been anything to worry about, I would have told you."

"But they said the ratings…"

"You and Josh are the backbone of the show," Trish said firmly. "Together or not together, they're damn lucky to have you both still on board in the third season. You're hot property right now. You could have thanked them kindly and jumped right into your movie career, but you haven't. You've been loyal to them."

I nodded. Trish sure sounded fired up.

"Okay, well, thanks for the heads up. It's exciting," I smiled, to no one but myself. "I'm finally going to be a movie star!"

"Kiddo?" Trish said. "You were *born* to be a movie star."

APRIL 1st

Riley and I are over. Oh, how I wish it had just been some cruel April Fool's Day prank...
"I don't understand what you want from me," I'd said, as I ran my fingers through my hair in exasperation. Riley sighed, glanced around the restaurant, then held my gaze.
"I want you to be my girlfriend."
"That's what I am! Is this because we don't see each other much?"
Riley shook his head, but I continued.
"Because if it is then, I'm afraid I can't do anything to change the situation. Work schedules are *so* beyond my control, and yours too. You're an actor. You should understand better than anyone."
"I do. It's not that."
"Then what is it?"
We were quiet as I contemplated the fact that we were arguing in the middle of a restaurant, and

that I didn't know what was making him so mad at me. Or what had made him travel thousands of miles to see me.
"It's got something to do with Josh."
I didn't quite hear what he said, so I asked him to repeat himself.
"I *said*, it has something to do with Josh," he repeated, this time with more exasperation in his voice.
I was confused. And surprised.
"What? What has this got to do with him?"
Riley closed his eyes, sat a little forward in his seat, then opened them again.
"You and Josh spend like, 24 hours a day together, and I guess… I guess I'd be lying if I said it didn't bother me."
"Why does that bother you? We're just friends."
"Are you?"
"Yes! God, yes."
I was still wearing that creased eyebrow expression of confusion, and he just looked kind of desperate, like he needed to get his point across.
"Because I just get this vibe from you. And him. Like you have some kind of sacred bond that I could never compete with."
"You're not supposed to compete with this. Josh is my friend. You are my *boy*-friend. There's a difference, and I like you both *because* you're different."
"But I can't be your friend too?"
"You're…"
"I just get the impression that I'm…being used. Like, I'm good for all the physical aspects of a relationship but anything intellectual, or friendly,

that's Josh's field."
Riley's tone was becoming a little more sarcastic and that was annoying.
"Look, I'm sorry if you feel that way. But what I love about our relationship is that it's fun."
Riley kind of rolled his eyes, but I continued on regardless.
"And it's not just 'a bit of fun', before you start thinking that."
He snapped his eyes to look at me.
"So, go on then."
"What?"
"How would you define our relationship?"
That kind of stumped me. I stared across the room in thought. I knew I had to come up with something quickly because *not* saying something might be worse than saying anything at all.
"It's... like... In a committed relationship, there's so much stress involved, so much worrying about the future. And I like that we don't have that."
"You don't think we have a future, is that what you're trying to say?" Riley challenged and I shook my head.
"No..."
"Then what, Beccy?"
"I just think we have the perfect set-up. Yes, ideally I'd like to see you more but other than that..."
Riley was looking away again, disbelief and even a little disinterest on his face. I sighed with exasperation.
"What? What is it you specifically hate about our relationship, Riley?"
He turned and looked me dead in the eye.
"The fact that I only get your body and not your

mind. That's what bugs me."
I couldn't help but let out an ironic laugh.
"I can't believe you're saying this! *I'm* the girl. You should be all for a no strings attached relationship."
"Well, I'm not. And I'm glad you find this to be such a big joke."
Riley stood up and walked past me. I sighed and threw a $20 bill on the table, then grabbed my bag and jacket and headed for the door. Riley had already breezed through it and I pushed on the door, tugging my jacket on at the same time. He'd gone left, and I followed him.
"Wait! Riley, stop!"
He did. He turned, folded his arms and waited.
"What?"
"You can't just leave. We have to finish this," I pleaded.
He looked at me with big eyes and I sighed.
"One way or another, we have to finish this."
He paused, thought about it, sighed and ran his fingers through his hair.
"I want you to back off from Josh."
I just looked at him and let out a small puff of air.
"Fine," I said. "And how do you expect me to do that?"
"I don't know," Riley returned. "Just…don't be with him all the time."
"Okay, fine. I'll hang out with him a little less. *That*, I can do."
Riley went to smile triumphantly but I cut him off.
"What about the fact that we live together? That'll make it pretty difficult for us to avoid each other, don't you think?"
Riley rolled his eyes.

"Don't even get me started on the sleeping arrangements..."
I wide-eyed him and he dived straight in.
"You and Josh live together! He gets to sleep with you every night, in *both* your apartments. I'm lucky if I even get to see you once a month!"
"He doesn't *sleep* with me..." I began weakly. "He sleeps on the sofa."
"Which is completely ridiculous," Riley argued. "Why would he still be doing that if he wasn't still into you? And *you* could have moved out months ago and got your own place. The fact is, you choose to still live together. You're okay with it, and unsurprisingly, so is he. It's just your boyfriend that inconveniences you because he can't deal with what, by anyone else's standards, is just a completely absurd situation."
I couldn't really argue with that. It *was* absurd, from an outsider's point of view. But somehow, for Josh and I specifically, it made sense. More than that, even, we hadn't questioned it. Not since we first split up. The more we became friends, the less of an issue it had become. But apparently, it was still a big issue for someone.
"I don't like it," Riley concluded, "and I doubt anyone else would either."
"The fact of the matter is," I stated calmly, "that Josh and I have lives that intertwine, be that because we choose or don't choose. We live together because we want to. We work together because we have to."
Riley rolled his eyes and I felt myself raring up in defence of myself.
"Riley, stop that! If I was to do everything you said, if I distanced myself from him, if I got my own

apartment for God’s sake, none of that would make any difference because we play a couple on Davey's Crowd! We have to kiss and make out for the cameras. I can't stop that. We don't choose that..."
"I know!"
"Then what?! What can I possibly do to distance myself from him? I can't change my life and I can't change his."
Riley sighed and shrugged.
"Maybe you're right. But I have a problem with you two being the way you are and I guess... I guess this problem isn't going to go away."
We stood opposite each other, both sensing the inevitable. I shivered in the wind as he stepped closer and placed his hands on my cheeks. Bringing his face a little closer to mine, and bending his knees to be on eye-level, he said softly,
"I know that this isn't a big deal for you, but it is for me. And if there's no way we can fix this, then...well, I guess we should call it a day."
He removed his hands and stepped away. I just gazed at him in a daze.
"But I've done so much for you," I said in a small voice. "I broke up with Josh for you. And now you want me to lose him as my friend too? What you're asking me to do... It's just not reasonable. You're asking me to break up with my best friend."
Riley just gazed back, saying a silent 'yes'. I took a deep breath then sighed as tears began to twinkle in my eyes and my throat began to tighten.
"I can't break off my friendship with Josh. I just can't."
Riley nodded and sighed, running his hand through his hair again.

"You can't, or you won't?"
I paused then simply and regretfully replied,
"I won't."
And Riley walked away. He walked away, turned the corner and disappeared out of sight. And he didn't look back once.

***

That night I saw Josh. Or rather, he came back to our apartment where I was sitting staring out of the window. Curled up in my pyjamas, hugging my knees tightly, with gentle radio music playing in the background, I'd been sitting in that window seat for hours.
"Hey, Beccy," he said as he closed the door. "God, it's cold out there."
I didn't ignore him as such, I just didn't reply. I listened as he took off his coat and hung it up, then pulled off his shoes and trudged over to me. He placed his icy hands on my cheeks and I jerked away from him with a scolding expression. Then, rather than say anything, I looked back out of the window. It was dark, but I could see all the lights from the other windows and the lampposts. The coldness outside made condensation on the inside, and I felt glad to be where I was.
Josh blew on his hands to warm them up and apologised. Then he touched my back and said, "You okay? You have a seriously mopey face."
I said nothing. I had no energy left to respond, not even with a shrug.
"You in an 'I don't want to speak' mood?"
Oh, how well he knew me. But rather than be

touched, it just made me think about Riley. And that made me sad. And confused. Josh sighed.
"Okay, fine. I'm going to the little boys' room, but when I come back, you're going to tell me what's wrong. Aren't you?"
Silence.
"I'll take that as a yes."
He went off and I closed my eyes, letting my head fall against the window. Was Josh really that important that I couldn't even have a boyfriend? Was Riley the exception, or would all my future boyfriends feel threatened by our relationship?
"Right," Josh said, walking towards me and sitting next to my feet. "Tell me everything. From the beginning."
I said nothing. I just stared out of the window. Patiently he waited, but I still said nothing. Then he rested his hand on my knee. I pulled away from his touch and he sensed it. He sighed.
"What have I done? I've hardly even seen you today, but I must have done something…"
Silence.
"Oh, c'mon! How can I grovel and make things up if you won't even tell me what I've done wrong?!"
I cleared my throat and very quietly said,
"You haven't done anything wrong."
Josh looked blankly at me then held his shoulders in a shrug.
"So what is it?"
He thought about it then smiled, leaning over to tickle my middle. I wriggled away as he teased,
"Is it boyfriend troubles? Is Riley refusing to put out?"
I sighed (he didn't know how cutting he was being)

and eyed him to leave me alone. He pulled away and sat quietly, just looking at me. Then it dawned on him and he started to slowly sit up straighter.
"You didn't… you guys didn't… break up?"
I said nothing and he sighed.
"You guys broke up, didn't you? God, I'm so sorry."
He paused then added,
"What happened?"
I sighed and stared harder out of the window.
"You don't have to tell me if…" he began.
"It was because of you."
Josh stared at me, confused, with creased eyebrows.
"Me? What did I do?"
I sighed and looked at him. He looked almost apologetic, wanting to know what he'd done and how he could fix it. His green-brown eyes were wide with disconcert and I just knew he was concerned about me in a way that not many other people could match.
"Nothing, really. Riley just… I guess he was jealous of our relationship. He doesn't like how close we are, how much time we spend together, other little stuff…"
"Like what?"
"Like us still living together and stuff. And us just being together all the time."
He nodded slowly, then rubbed his eyes with his hand. Then he looked at me and shrugged his shoulders.
"I'm sorry. I had no idea."
"Me either," I said, looking back out of the window.
We didn't say much for a while, and Josh leaned his back against the window, clasping his hands

together and slouching. My mind was racing with thoughts, but it was all so confusing. Finally, Josh spoke.

"Do you think if I talked to him…"

I sighed and sat up a little bit, as did he.

"No, Josh. The point is, Riley doesn't want to understand it. He just wanted me to be with him all the time, and not have any friends who are guys, and…"

"I think you're missing the point here, Beccy."

I was so surprised, I just *had* to listen to Josh. He was defending Riley?!

"I don't think he's jealous of *all* the guys. He's just jealous of us. I think to an outsider - I mean, anyone that's not us - we do seem really tight and like, best friends. And the fact that we still live together is pretty unusual, but…"

He reached over and stroked my cheek, just as Riley had. This time, I closed my eyes.

"Beccy? I don't think Riley is being as abnormally demanding as you think he is. I think deep down you know where's coming from."

I nodded and opened my eyes, but I looked to the side of Josh and out of the window. He lowered his hand to rest on my knee.

"Your eyes don't look red," he noted.

"That's because I haven't been crying."

"I would have thought…"

"Me too," I said, and Josh sat back next to my feet, but facing me. We were quiet for a while.

"Why didn't you cry?"

I shrugged.

"I guess I was mad. That he was being so unreasonable."

Josh nodded and we fell quiet again. Then I realised what the real reason was and Josh saw it in my face.
"What?"
"Nothing."
"You thought of something, so tell me."
I paused for a while then breathed deeply in and tucked my hair behind my ears. Finally, I caught his eyes with mine.
"I think deep down I knew that although I lost my boyfriend, I still have my best friend. And I guess that's more important to me."
I looked out of the window again and said a little quieter,
"*You're* more important to me."
Josh couldn't help himself. He smiled and leaned over, enveloping me in a tight hug. I held him closely and breathed him in, my eyes closed. He stroked my hair and sighed.
"Beccy, you'll never lose me. I'm not going anywhere."
I pulled away but we kept ourselves entangled, as he pushed my hair from my face and looped it behind my ear. His eyes darted across my face before coming to settle on my eyes.
"Josh?" I asked and he nodded with a small smile.
"What if all my boyfriends are like this? What if I fall in love with someone but they hate us?"
Josh cocked his head and shrugged.
"I guess I'll have to be the person you fall in love with then."
I closed my eyes and let out a sad laugh. Josh pulled me close to him again and I rested my hands on his back, closing my eyes as my head nestled

perfectly into his shoulder.

***

As I lay in bed that night, my mind drifted back to Riley. What he was asking of me wasn't unreasonable, I concluded, but it was impossible. This dynamic of ours was unique, there was no doubt about that, and as Josh had pointed out, no one but us would ever understand it. The thing was, I wasn't sure I understood it myself. Were we friends? Were we more? What if Josh was who I was supposed to be with, my soulmate? But then again, what if he wasn't, and he was destined to be my friend, but the actual love of my life dismissed me *because* of Josh?

I decided my entire life was fast becoming one big April Fool's joke…and I really wasn’t laughing.

APRIL 11th

I closed the door of the trailer behind me. It made a soft slamming sound, on account of the flimsy material it was made of, but I knew it was shut securely. I put the two brown paper bags onto the fold-out table and whirled my scarf off, dropping it onto the deep red velvet seating. I paused and looked along the empty trailer. This was home now.

I'd arrived in Montreal, Canada, to begin filming Irresponsible Actions only yesterday morning. I'd said an emotional goodbye to the cast of Davey's Crowd, most notably Josh, who seemed sad to be waving me off for four weeks. Even though we weren't together - and hadn't been now for the best part of half a year - this would in fact be the longest time we'd spent apart since we first met. I knew I'd miss him, of course, but I was filled with a sense of independence and an overwhelming feeling of

excitement at being on my first movie shoot.
The arrival, then, had been a bit of a reality check. With no Trish either (as I was now over 18, she was no longer legally obliged to accompany me as my guardian), I'd arrived at the airport to find myself hailing a cab to the set, clutching only a piece of paper with the contact number of the assistant to the producer, Evelyn. She'd given me directions to the location, which was north of the main city, and once we'd finally been introduced, she'd shown me to my trailer, given me a finished script and a call-sheet for the following day, and told me that someone would come and get me at 7am sharp in the morning. As the door closed behind her, and an eerie kind of quiet fell in the trailer, I realised that I wasn't just on my own - I was alone.
The first night had been very strange. Unnerving, even. I'd checked the door was shut and locked about a hundred times before I got into bed (lumpy and uncomfortable) and lay staring up at the ceiling. The shoot itself, although funded by a major studio, was aiming for a serious audience, more like an independent feature, and as such, it had gone for a more 'low-budget' feel. Which meant *all* costs were being kept low, including apparently, accommodation.
But the next morning, as I unpacked my stuff and set about making the place feel a little more like someone lived there, I began to settle in. It really wasn't that bad…
There'd been a knock at the door just as I was tying up my shoelaces. I went over and opened the door. Evelyn. A friendly face, it seemed, and my only one so far.

"Hi, how are you doing?" she asked.
I nodded and smiled warmly.
"Good, thanks. Just getting settled in."
"I just got word from Mr. Rose that he'd like you to come to his trailer as soon as possible."
"Oh, does he now?" I said, with a raised eyebrow. We'd had a read-through back in Manhattan last week, with Ray the director, Randy Milton from Young Bros., several of the producers and some of the financiers. It was the first time I'd met my other co-stars, and I'd really liked them, especially Jess Newton, who was playing my character's best friend, Trina. But I hadn't met Oliver Rose. Oliver had been 'unfortunately engaged' and had been 'unable to attend'. This elusive self-centred individual was not making the best first impression on me - and that was before we'd even met. And now he was summoning me to his trailer like some sort of Lord?
I so wanted to tell Evelyn to tell Oliver where to… But I didn't. I took a calm, professional breath and nodded with a sweet smile.
"Sure," I charmed. "Let me just grab my stuff."
I put my heavy woollen coat over my jeans and plain top ensemble and buttoned it up. I grabbed my scarf and my woolly hat and pulled them on. Montreal in March was unforgiving when it came to the weather. I put my phone in my pocket and pulled the door shut behind me, locking it with the solitary key that was now all I had in the way of possessions. I placed that in my other pocket and we were off.
Oliver's trailer was a short walk from mine. Was it my imagination or was it bigger? And a little

shinier? The boy sure knew how to pull the strings in this business - he had everyone, including the tight-fisted finance department, bending over backwards to accommodate him. Evelyn led me to the door, but stopped to answer a crackled message on her walkie-talkie.
"Do you mind if I leave you here? I just have to go and sort out a few things," she explained.
I looked nervously up at the door then regained my composure. If Oliver thought he could intimidate *me*, then he had another thing coming…
"Go ahead. I'll be fine."
Evelyn nodded and smiled as she hurried away and I practically stormed up the steps to hammer firmly on the door. I took in a slow, deep breath, forcing myself to stay strong in the face of whatever bristly, arrogant attitude I was about to come face to face with.
"Come in," I heard him call. Charming. The guy wasn't even going to answer the door. I pushed it open and stepped inside, looking around.
He was standing in the kitchen, stirring a cup of coffee. Wearing a yellow t-shirt over baggy jeans, he had a pen sticking out of his mouth which he was chewing as he looked down at the script that lay on the kitchen counter. I took his moment of self-absorption to take a good, hard look at my new co-star.
He was taller than me, although only by a little. He was slim, his t-shirt clinging to his straight up and down waist. His hair was a mass of dark curls, unkempt and messy, and as he finally looked along the trailer in my direction, I could see why he'd been named Teen Talk's Heartthrob of the Year.

Oliver was beautiful to look at. His curls gave him an angelic, playful sort of air, and teamed with his big, brown eyes and almost baby-faced features, he was one very pretty man. And he was looking right at me.
"I'm sorry," he startled, his formal British accent new to my ears. "You must be Rebecca."
He left his cup on the side and came towards me, holding out his hand.
"It's a pleasure to meet you," he smiled.
That accent. Wow. It was all kinds of gorgeous.
"It's nice to *finally* meet you," I replied, a little heavy on the emphasis, as I shook his hand.
Oliver rolled his eyes.
"I know, I know. What a way to make a first impression, right? My schedule has been an absolute nightmare."
He crossed his hands in front of him resolutely.
"But that's no excuse. I'm so sorry I couldn't make the read-through last week. I hear it went well though, no?"
I felt like I was in Mary Poppins or something. Except this was more 'dashingly handsome debonair' than 'chimney-sweep'. Now he was standing so close to me, I was a little overwhelmed by his looks too. He was the whole package - no wonder he always got what he wanted. King of the charmers, no doubt...
I nodded and pushed my hair behind my ears, taking a step back.
"Yeah, it was good. I think the higher-up's were impressed."
"That's the most important thing, right? To make sure the men with the money-bags are happy," he

said with a smile, returning to his coffee.
"Would you like one? A tea, perhaps?" he asked.
This was all too much. Was he putting it on? I couldn't help but smile and he noticed.
"What?"
"Oh, it's nothing. It's just... Tea? Really? Isn't that like, a bit of cliché?"
Oliver rolled his eyes and smiled, pushing his hand up the back of his neck and giving his curls a shake.
"Yes, I suppose it is. But all clichés are founded in some truth, and I *love* tea," he confessed with a smile, coming towards me. He sat at the table and I sat opposite him, instinctively.
"So..." he said, finally getting his own chance to give me a once-over. I watched his eyes watching me and I felt a little uneasy.
"Rebecca," he stated.
"Beccy's fine," I corrected, and he nodded.
"Beccy, then. I suppose I just wanted to meet you before we got started on the shoot."
"So that's why you summoned me..."
Oliver frowned.
"Summoned you?" he asked in a clipped tone.
I nodded.
"Evelyn said you wanted to see me in your trailer as soon as possible," I explained. "It was kind of like being summoned..."
His frown deepened.
"I'm so sorry," he said. "I didn't mean it to come across like that. I really just asked her to ask you..."
"It's fine," I said, waving my hand dismissively. It had only been a few minutes, but I was already realising that my initial ideas about Oliver had

been wrong. The young, handsome but casual kind of guy sitting opposite me wasn't matching up to the big, bad spoilt prima donna image I'd constructed in my mind.
"So…" I said, glancing around the trailer. "You said your schedule's been busy. What have you just come from?"
"I literally just finished promotion for Teen Crusader: American Adventure."
I nodded and smiled.
"What's that, the fourth...?"
He nodded.
"And to be quite honest, I'll be glad when this contract is complete."
I simply raised an eyebrow at him and he rolled his eyes, leaning forwards as he grasped hold his cup (which I now realised had tea in it, not coffee).
"I hope I don't sound ungrateful because believe you me, I know how much this franchise has given me. A career, for a start. But it's just…it's been back to back. Movie, promotion, movie, promotion, it's never-ending. And I have absolutely no say over the character, and I don't know if you've seen any of them, but they've had me doing some pretty ridiculous stuff."
I smirked.
"It's not exactly the 'coolest' of movie franchises…" I replied tentatively.
"It's for kids, and they love it," Oliver shrugged frankly. "But I'm 21 now, and I've just…I've kind of had enough of it all, to be honest."
I nodded.
"I know how you feel."
"You do?"

"Well, I mean, I don't have some box office busting trilogy of movies behind me or anything…" I said with a smile. "But last year, I got real obsessed with trying to change how people saw me. I'm on this show, you see…"
"The teen one? Something…'Crowd'?" Oliver said, pointing his finger at me. I grinned.
"Yes. Davey's Crowd."
"That's it. I've had absolutely no time to watch any kind of TV in, God, what feels like forever, but I did read an interview in a magazine on the flight here. You guys just did some kind of bomb scare episode or something…"
I nodded.
"I'm impressed."
Oliver smiled the most charming of smiles at me, his eyes gently creasing at the corners.
"Well, I did have a spare five minutes before they put my movie on as the in-flight entertainment, so…"
I gasped and he let out a laugh. I told him about the show, and how my character Casey was this straight-laced, all-American kind of girl, and that I'd been so happy to have landed this role because Jessica was going to be so different. Oliver knew exactly how I felt, as his character was a drug dealer, and well, the Teen Crusader most definitely wasn't.
"I feel like this is my chance, you know, to show people what I can really do," he said sincerely to me. "That I can really act."
Leaning forwards, hanging on his every well-spoken word, I could only nod in heartfelt agreement. He smiled and slammed his hand onto

the table.
"Well, come on then Rebecca..."
"Beccy."
"*Beccy,*" he corrected, sliding off the seat and standing up. "Let's go show them what we're made of."

***

I couldn't have imagined just how easy it was going to be to generate chemistry with a complete stranger. I also could never have imagined that I would have been able to do that with Oliver. I'd spent months imagining what he was going to be like, preparing myself for the worst, assuring myself that I could get through it, no matter how much of a jerk he turned out to be... And by the end of the first day, we were joking around and laughing together like we'd known each other for a lifetime.
"Do you have food?" he'd asked me, as we walked back to our trailers. I yawned and shook my head.
"No."
"How far do you think it is to the nearest shop?"
"What kind of a shop?"
He looked at me in confusion.
"A shop that sells food..."
"You mean a grocery store?"
Oliver nodded and pointed at me.
"That's the one."
"I think we're going to have fun with this...." I smiled teasingly. I stopped and pointed down at the floor.
"What's this?" I asked.

"The pavement," he replied.
I grinned.
"It's called the sidewalk," I corrected.
Oliver arched an eyebrow at me and folded his arms.
"Maybe in your country."
"Well, we're..." I began, before pausing. He pointed at me and grinned.
"Ha! We're not even *in* your country."
"Well, it's still called the same out here. Next..."
I turned around and pointed across the road.
"What's that?"
"A petrol station," he said.
"*No...*"
"Wait a minute," he said, his eyes widening. "I know this one. It's a...service station?"
"Yeah, sure. Close enough."
Oliver rolled his eyes but smiled despite himself.
"And it sells...?" I asked.
"Petrol."
We both looked at each other and said in unison, "Gas!"
He screwed up his nose.
"Look here, lady, if you have some personal hygiene issues you want to let me know about..."
I gasped and shoved myself into him with my elbow bent. As I found myself giggling, I realised we were going to get along just fine.

***

And so this morning, as I returned from the nearby grocery store and began to unpack the food, a sense of well-being began to rise inside me. I can totally

do this, I told myself, before hearing a knock at the door.
"Come in," I called, closing the refrigerator door. It was Oliver. He bounded inside, blowing on his hands and hunching his shoulders as the door slammed (softly) shut behind him.
"It's bloody freezing out there."
"Well, why aren't you wearing a coat?" I asked, looking at his hooded sweatshirt.
"I figured you'd have the heating on in here but…" he said, looking at the half-empty paper bag, "I see you've already been out. To the *grocery store.*"
I smirked at him and he flashed me a charming smile.
"Anyway," he said, backing up and sitting down on the sofa, reaching for the TV remote, "I figured you might like some company. We're not due on set until eleven."
I reached into the bag and pulled out a carton of orange juice, looking over at Oliver as he kicked off his trainers and settled himself comfortably into the seat. Watching the TV intently, his eyes fixed on the screen, he didn't see me smile. Or sigh with contentment. So much for having a co-star I couldn't get on with - he'd become my new best friend overnight.

APRIL 20th

"Here."
I raised my eyes to look into his. They were stricken, panicked.
"Just take it!"
He pressed a small package into my hand and forcibly curled my fingers around it. As he held my fist inside both his hands, he stared hard into my eyes.
"Don't let anyone know you have these."
I nodded. The bell rang and the corridor was suddenly filled with students, rushing to their next class. I pushed the package into the pockets of my jeans and watched him walk away, disappearing into the chaos.
"And...CUT!"
I looked for Oliver to re-emerge and when he did, he was smiling and ruffling his curls. I grinned at him as Ray came to meet both of us in the middle

of the set. All around us, people busied themselves in preparation for the next take, should it be required.
"Great," Ray said. "Are you both happy with that?"
Oliver and I exchanged a look and nodded at each other.
"Then let's move on…" Ray said, backing away before turning and yelling out,
"Let's move on, people!"
Oliver came closer to me as I removed the package from my pocket and looked at it.
"What is it supposed to be?" I asked, looking through the plastic wrapping at the small, white pills.
"Ecstasy, I should think."
I snapped my eyes to look at him but he smiled.
"No, no, I'm not harbouring some secret drug problem," he said, as one of the director's assistants came rushing up to me and took away the prop.
Oliver and I turned and headed in the general direction that everyone else seemed to be moving.
"So then how do you…"
"I was offered one. At an after-party for the first Crusader movie."
I looked at him in shock.
"Seriously?"
He nodded, pushing his hands into the pockets of Cody's rugged leather jacket.
"Yep. I was 17 at the time, and this producer came up to me and said…"
Oliver looked at me with a sneery smile and said in his best American accent (which was actually pretty good),
"Here, kid. Don't say I never did nothin' for ya."

I shook my head.
"That's outrageous."
"Isn't it?" he nodded. "Especially when you think about the studio that makes the movies. I mean, it's supposed to be this family-orientated, sweet as apple pie place, and they're offering this kid Class A drugs."
I let out a sigh and we came to a stop as about forty people tried to squeeze through a set of double doors.
"So you haven't…?" he enquired and I shook my head.
"No. And thankfully, I haven't been put in the difficult position you were. Although I know it goes on. Trish and my parents have warned me, and my friend Jenna told me she got invited to share a line of coke with one of the producers from her TV show."
Oliver raised an eyebrow.
"Did she get fired?"
"My friend? No. She didn't do it."
"No, the producer, I mean."
"Jenna didn't say anything," I explained. "She was too scared of losing her job. But she said it made looking her in the eye pretty difficult after that."
Oliver and I were outside now, and Evelyn had managed to squeeze her way through the crush to find us.
"We're moving onto the parking lot scene," she said, flipping over the call-sheet she had attached to clipboard. "You ready for blocking on that?"
"I'd like to have another quick look at the script, if that's okay."
Oliver crossed his arms and shook his head.

"Not prepared for the scene?"
He began to tut and I narrowed my eyes at him.
"Actually, it's the opposite. I want to ensure I am *best* prepared for the scene, unlike some people round here, who are just coasting by on their good looks…"
His mouth dropped open and I grinned, taking the script from Evelyn and skimming over the words. I'd learnt these lines last night with…
"Jess."
I looked up to see Oliver raising his hand in greeting as our co-star came skipping towards us.
"Hey, you guys. How was the scene?" she asked. Her usually pretty light brown hair was scruffy and pulled up in an unkempt ponytail, and caked-on, smeared make-up was distorting her usually attractive face. She looked like someone using drugs, which was precisely the look that the hair and make-up department had been going for.
"Good. Do you need to check the script? Little Miss Unprepared here is hogging it but…"
"Take no notice of him, Jess," I said, keeping my eyes on the page. "He's causing trouble."
"You are *definitely* a trouble-maker," I heard Jess reply, a hint of flirtation in her voice. Oliver sure was charming and even though I was on the receiving end of some of his oh-so-witty banter, so far, I hadn't felt any stirrings of attraction. I glanced at him, smiling a bright smile back at Jess, and wondered why not. I thanked Evelyn for the script and handed it back to her, then reached into my pocket to check my phone. It was done more out of instinct than anything, and I realised this when the disappointment of having no messages panged my

heart.
Riley was history. He hadn't texted, he hadn't called, he'd just disappeared out of my life as quickly as he'd entered it. All I was left with was a feeling of unfinished business and unrequited love. It sucked not to be wanted by someone. Or missed at all, it seemed. I put my phone back and looked up at Jess and Oliver, who both looked at me.
"You coming?"
I nodded and followed them across to the parking lot, where a scruffy old Pontiac was sat, doors open, waiting for us.
"So," Ray said, as the three of us approached. "We're just waiting on lighting but other than that, I figured we'd go ahead and start blocking the scene. Jess, you're in the back. Cody, you're driving. *Obviously...*"
Ray looked at me.
"And Beccy, if you can be standing just to one side, we're gonna take the scene as if Cody's just pulled over."
The three of us nodded and got into position. Ray said 'From the top', but other than that, nothing else about this was anything like a real take. Blocking was purely a technical thing, to iron out any potential kinks (poor lighting, bad focus) before any actual time, money and energy was wasted on a real take. So we went through the scene a few times, stopping to allow the lighting guys to set up a new rig, but everything went without a hitch so it was onto the real thing.
"Set."
I took a deep breath and looked around. All the crew were in position but now, they were frozen.

"Roll sound."
There was a quiet pause before the sound mixer confirmed,
"Rolling."
I glanced at Ray, who was sitting behind a bank of monitors, and he raised his hand.
"Roll camera."
"Rolling," came the confirmation from the camera operator, who was standing only a few feet from me, the lens focussed right at me.
"Slate," Ray said.
The clapperboard was raised between me and the camera, and the slate operator called loudly,
"Scene six, take one!"
CLAP.
"And...action!" Ray yelled.
"Hey, sexy."
I leaned down and peered inside the car, where Oliver/Cody peered up at me, squinting in the fake sunshine of the lighting rig.
"Don't call me that," I sassed.
"You love it," he grinned. "Now...where's the stuff?"
I crossed my arms and looked down at him.
"And what 'stuff' is that?"
His face turned serious, sinister even. My own teasing smile disappeared from my face as he reached out and grabbed hold of my arm.
"Don't mess with me, little girl."
I winced in pain as his grip tightened and yanked my arm from him.
"If you want me to be your mule, Cody, then you'd better show me some God damn respect.
"*Keep*...your voice down," he threatened, and I

glanced around the parking lot (mostly at the crew, to be honest). I peered in the window.
"Is that…Trina?"
Oliver/Cody nodded.
"Is she…?" I asked.
"She's fine. And she's the least of your worries. Where's the stuff, Jess?"
I looked over my shoulder before reaching into my pocket and pulling out the package, which I'd put back in just before the take. I bent down at the car window and held it out between us. Oliver/Cody reached for it and I teasingly pulled it back. He stared at me, then half-smiled. He took hold of the package as he leaned closer to me and pressed his lips on mine.
I knew this scene was going to contain 'the kiss' and I'd tried not to make too big a deal out of it. But now here I was, kissing Oliver Rose…albeit for the cameras. His lips felt different. They weren't Riley's, sadly. And they weren't Josh's, which I'd become so used to. This was a screen kiss, for sure, but he was still pretty good at it.
Oliver/Cody stopped and flashed me a wicked grin.
"Thanks, baby," he said, sitting back in his seat, throwing the package onto the seat and pretending to drive away. I stepped back and pretended to watch him go, as the camera operator came rushing towards me for a close-up. I held a hurt, rejected expression on my face for a few moments, waiting for the inevitable…
"And cut! Check the gate!"
Oliver - back to being just Oliver - poked his head out of the window and peered up at me.

"How was it for you, my dear?" he charmed, his accent even more pronounced than usual. I reached up to touch my lips, then brushed my hair free from my face.
"It was okay, I suppose..."
"Ah, you loved it!" he grinned, and I let out a laugh, smiling down at him.
"Next time, I'm going to try it with tongues," he teased and I gasped, reaching in to jab him on the shoulder.
"You'd better not!" I warned.
He didn't. But takes two, three and four (to cover all possible camera angles) were just as enjoyable as the first.

***

I spent the rest of the afternoon in a little trailer, doing scenes for Davey's Crowd. The writers had managed to come up with the perfect solution to the absent Casey Bridges - an exchange trip to Paris. So all I had to do was film a few scenes with a webcam filter and record a few phonecalls (with Evelyn standing in as Josh, which was a little strange) and I was covered for the entire duration of filming. Easy.
"Are you missing your friends?" Evelyn asked me, as the cameraman transferred the footage onto a laptop to send on to the studio. I paused. Was I? I'd been so busy making new friends with Oliver and Jess that I'd barely even thought about Jared, Connor and Meghan. Josh, well, that was different. He occupied a very different place in my mind, and my heart. I'd missed him, though as each day

passed, the feeling definitely grew a little weaker.
"Yes," I chose to reply, realising that made me seem a lot less fickle and lot more loyal. Evelyn smiled.
"Well, we're nearly halfway through already. You'll be back before you know it."
It surprised me how unbothered I'd felt at hearing that.

MAY 3rd

My body lay pressed on top of his as I gazed down into his eyes. He looked up at me, happy and relaxed, and pushed some hair behind my ear. I reciprocated his touch with my own, moving my hand to stroke his cheek. I closed my eyes and smiled, letting my body fall onto his and press harder, as I lay my lips on his for a kiss. We kissed and kissed, his hands under my hair, on the back of my neck, pulling me forcefully into him. Our legs intertwined, I ran my hands up and down his slim waist before grabbing hold of him to steady myself. His kiss was intense.

With a parting smile, I rolled off him and lay beside him instead, staring up and squinting in the light. I raised my hand to cover my eyes then saw in my periphery vision that I was being offered something. I took the joint from him and held it between my lips, inhaling the smoke then slowly

exhaling, before closing my eyes and smiling a contented smile.
"And…CUT!"
I turned my head to look at Oliver, the harsh glare of the spotlight that had been standing in as sunshine leaving behind grey spots in my vision. I handed the joint back to him, and he handed it to the props girl, who extinguished it. It was only a herbal cigarette anyway.
"That was great, guys," Ray said, coming towards us. I sat up and smoothed my hands down my hair. Oliver propped himself up on his elbow.
"What are you guys thinking? Is there anything you want to do before we move on?" Ray asked.
I looked at Oliver and he arched a flirty eyebrow at me.
"Well…" he said, rubbing his chin with a curled finger, "I was thinking perhaps at this stage in the proceedings that Cody might try to move things forwards. Push his luck a bit."
"Oliver might push his luck, don't you mean?" I smirked at him.
"What did you have in mind?" Ray asked, with genuine curiosity. Oliver grinned.
"Ah, I'm just kidding. Nah, I think we've got it covered."
"Yes," I agreed, as Ray looked at me. "Please don't make me do any more hot and heavy scenes with this guy. I really am digging deep in my reserves to generate such a believable performance."
An understanding smile spread across Ray's face. He was starting to get the rapport Oliver and I had, which was one based on mutual teasing, with a heavy dose of sarcasm. He stood up and looked to

the crew, whirling his finger round.
"Okay, people!" he called. "I think that's a wrap on…"
"It's raining!" someone called out. I watched as the crew went into overdrive, packing up equipment and throwing things into cases. Even at lightning speed, the dark and heavy clouds had rolled in quicker than expected for everyone and the rain was truly coming down.
I shrieked and jumped up, pulling the blanket up as Oliver stepped off it.
"What should I grab?" he asked me.
"Anything!" I replied, and he rushed over to me, throwing his arms around me as I staggered backwards to absorb the impact.
"I got you!" he said. "Don't worry, everyone! I've got the star, she's fine."
I giggled as he reached down and wrapped the picnic blanket tight around my arms, pinning them to my side, as he manhandled me in the direction of the nearby trees. We'd set up the 'make out' scene in the middle of a farmer's field and once we hit the boundaries, and we were under the canopy of the trees, Oliver and I turned to watch the chaos as the crew split and scattered, carrying equipment either towards the trees like us or to the cars parked along the road.
As I stood in Oliver's embrace, my wet hair stuck to my cheeks, I smiled. I felt safe in his arms and I gazed up at him as he looked across the field. He was incredibly handsome, almost too pretty for his own good. His curls were now wet, the springy tendrils framing his face, and I had *such* an urge to reach up and ruffle them. He was beyond cute.

Oliver looked down at me and smiled and we held each other's gaze as strongly as he held me in his arms. *This* was a moment. It was upon me before I'd had time to anticipate it but being right in the midst of it, my heart and mind racing with possibilities and hope and anticipation, I knew we had crossed a line that we hadn't crossed before. But just as soon as it had transpired, it was gone. Oliver looked back into the field and I lowered my gaze, turning to rest my head against his chest. I felt him give me a squeeze and wondered what that meant. Then I began to wonder why our moment had ended so quickly. We had chemistry, there was no doubt about that. Hell, the studio were practically doing back-flips at the dailies. 'You can't underestimate the importance of a connection between your two romantic leads,' Ray had told me, 'without it, the whole movie falls apart'. Well, we had that connection for sure. We'd had it right from the very first meeting we'd had in Oliver's trailer, and day by day, late night by late night, it had grown. And here we were, on our final day of shooting, with our arms wrapped around each other, having just had a moment that wasn't generated for the cameras...and it had fizzled out like a damp squib. Maybe it had been all that rain, which was still coming down heavy.
I was attractive to him, surely? I was fun to be around and we got on really well and like I said, we had chemistry. We flirted. I mean, it never really went anywhere but we joked and we teased and we seemed to have absolutely no boundaries when it came to physical contact. We'd cuddle and he'd given me piggybacks, and sometimes I'd sit on

his lap between takes, although more often than not he'd jokingly sit on mine. We'd kissed, *a lot*, and although that had been for the cameras, and my mind had been on the job and not on other things, it had felt pretty convincing nonetheless. So why wasn't I feeling it? Or more importantly, why wasn't *he* feeling it?

We rejoined the crew and everyone headed back to the lot, our central location and general hub, before splitting off again for lunch.

"You coming?" Oliver asked.

"Where?"

"To mine."

"Uh…I think I'm going to head back to mine, actually," I said, as nonchalantly as I could manage. I didn't want to give anything away, nor did I want there to be a shift in our dynamic. I really, really liked our dynamic. Oliver nodded and shrugged, walking backwards away from me.

"Catch you later then," he pointed and I smiled at him before taking the three steps into my trailer and closing the door behind me. Alone. And it actually felt kind of good.

I made myself some lunch and watched some random afternoon TV then, when Evelyn came knocking with my call to set, I jumped up happily to follow her. The time away from Oliver had made me appreciate just how special whatever it was we had. I'd missed him, even though we'd only been apart for an hour or so. I'd come to rely on him for everything - companionship, friendship, and everything in between. He was my one-man support system and I realised I'd have been an idiot to throw that away for some angsty confused

feelings. What did it matter what we were if it worked?
When I saw him standing by the camera monitor, I smiled. When he looked at me and gave me a flirty wink, I grinned. And we were right back on track.

***

"So you're telling me there's absolutely nothing going on between you two?"
I slicked my lips with lip gloss and moistened them together. I turned and looked at Jess, who was sitting in the living area of my trailer, tapping her feet impatiently against the floor.
"Like I said," I shrugged, throwing the lip gloss into my bag and zipping it up, "I'm not going to dwell on what we have or don't have or could have. Oliver and I get on great and that's all that really matters."
I walked down from my bedroom to the living area as Jess stood up.
"Fair enough," she shrugged back, tugging on the low side-ponytail she was wearing. "It's just, you know, you have to give me some credit. I've been working alongside you both for a whole month and I've seen things…"
A smile spread across her face, followed quickly by one across mine.
"Look, I'm tired of trying to figure out my feelings for Josh and Riley. The last thing I need is to throw Oliver into the mix."
"No matter how cute and charming and British he is?" she said, her smile turning into a playful smirk.
I tipped my head to one side and raised any

eyebrow at her in response. She rolled her eyes and raised both her hands.
"Fine!" she said. "Let's just go and have fun tonight."
I nodded and followed behind her as she headed towards the door.
"Exactly," I agreed, placing my hands onto her shoulders. "It's the wrap party. We made it! Do you realise we actually *made* it?"
I closed the door behind me and locked it before skipping down to join her. She linked her arm into mine and we walked along, out of the lot and towards the road, where we knew our taxi was waiting.
"I've had so much fun," she confessed and I grinned at her, giving her arm a squeeze with my own.
"Me too. We really, really need to stay in touch."
"Oh girlfriend, don't think you can get rid of me that easily. I'm a friend for life!"
We smiled at each other and I hoped she was right. Jess had replaced Steph, Meghan, my Mom, my sisters, hell, every female in my life that I depended on for heartfelt chats, boy-related chats, industry and acting-related chats, idle chats... In the same way as with Oliver, I felt like I'd known Jess my whole life, not just four weeks. Apparently being away from home and working on a movie set acted like a magnifying glass for relationships.
Everything was intensified. And now here we were, on our way into Montreal city centre, for our final night and a wrap-party that was promised as the party to end all parties. I felt a mixture of relief and satisfaction, at knowing my time on Irresponsible Actions had come to an end, but also

a sense of loss, sadness and even a little fear. I'd been in a bit of a bubble, with my regular life on hold. It seemed a far away prospect, and what would it hold for me once I returned? Would Davey's Crowd seem dull and unchallenging? Would being Casey Bridges seem like a step back now that I'd pushed myself to be Jessica Albright? Was Riley waiting for me, was Josh, or had they both moved on? I wondered how long my working visa would last - Montreal seemed like a safe haven right now.

We arrived at the bar just before nine. It was called Casa de la Mama and it looked pretty small from the outside. Jess and I went in and looked around. The place was already heaving, and I recognised many of the faces as crew. Wondering where Oliver was, his handsome smiling face popped up right in front of us and, flinging his arms around us, he pulled us both into him with a surprised yelp.

"My girls are here!" he declared, giving us both a quick kiss on the cheek. He stepped between us and turned around, holding out both his arms to us. We all linked up and walked across the bar, probably wearing matching beaming smiles. Being around Oliver felt like a guaranteed good time, even if the bar was dated. And come to think of it, so was the music. I noticed a cramped dance-floor over to one side with a big shiny disco-ball hanging over it.

"So this place is...*interesting*," I noted, looking around. Oliver held three fingers up towards the barman, but Lord only knows what he'd ordered us. He looked at me, then around the bar.

"Yeah, it's kind of retro, isn’t it?"
"I'll say," Jess said, pulling her feet up off the sticky floor. "The carpets clearly haven’t been cleaned since the Seventies..."
Oliver rolled his eyes.
"Come on, you divas. Who cares about the décor when you have drinks…" he said, taking three shot glasses and lining them up in front of him, "good music and fantastically handsome company?"
"Good point," I grinned, nudging him with my arm before reaching for a glass. Jess stood the other side of Oliver and took hers.
"To living up to the movie's name," Oliver said, holding his glass high. "To a night filled with irresponsible actions and wild behaviour!"
"Hell yeah!" Jess whooped, and I giggled as we clinked our glasses together and threw the liquid down our throats. Oh, how it burned. Oliver flashed me a wicked grin as he slammed his glass down on the bar and held out his hand to me.
"Shall we dance?" he asked, the formality of his British accent making the request seem all the more inviting.
I nodded, slipping my hand into his.
"You're next!" he pointed at Jess, and she pointed back at him. Then she gave me a knowing grin before turning back to the bar and ordering another drink. As Oliver led me onto the dance-floor, I began to wonder if the combination of the shoot coming to an end, plus copious amounts of alcohol, might make tonight a no-holds-barred kind of night. A 'whatever happens in Montreal stays in Montreal' kind of thing. Oliver turned to face me, backing into the middle of the crowd, and pulled

on my hand. As I bumped into him, our eyes locked onto each other and I felt a thrilling surge of energy. I was up for that.
Wow, that boy can dance. I had no idea. I figured he would be the kind of guy not to care about how he looked, perhaps - he was full of confidence and pretty self-assured. But I had no idea he'd actually have the moves to back that up. There was this disco song on, I think it must have been called 'Don't Take Away The Music' (that's the line they kept repeating), and I figured he'd be goofing around, throwing all kinds of shapes and being a bit of a joker with it. But he was *sexy* dancer. This was Swayze, not Travolta, and as he pulled me close to him, and we intertwined our bodies as we danced together to the beat, I realised that Oliver was still a bit of a mystery to me. Sure, we'd gotten to know each other pretty well, but this was a revelation. What other tricks and talents did he have up his sleeves?
"You dance really well," I complimented and he grinned at me before giving me a nonchalant shrug.
"It's just another string to my bow."
"Well, if you're all as handsome and charming and brilliant at dancing as this, then I'm thinking a move to London might be in order."
"Hey," he said, raising a finger.
"What?"
"Don't forget how good I am at making tea."
I nodded and smiled.
"That is true. I'm definitely getting into having a nice cup of Earl Grey in the morning," I said, putting on my best British accent. Oliver laughed.

"You know something?" he said, pulling me close. I gazed into his eyes, our noses almost touching.
"What?" I dared, with a flirty smile.
"I think you're the very best kind of people."
"Aww."
"No, I mean it," he said, running his hand through his curls. "You really are something quite different."
I smiled and nodded to myself, then patted his chest with my hand.
"You're good people too."
"I am?" he asked, and we looked at each other.
There was that locked-on intense gaze again. And his arms were around me. Moment number two.
"You know you are," I charmed and his smile turned into a grin.
"Well at least now I know that not *all* Americans are stupid..."
I gasped and he laughed, and I playfully pushed him away. He came close again and wrapped his arms around me. We hugged each other tightly, rocking from side to side. My heart was full of love for him in that, our third and very best moment, but I knew it was the kind of love you felt for a friend. A close and cherished friend, but a friend nonetheless.
Not that Jess believed me at all, of course, as I made my way back to the bar.
"Okay, so now I *know* you're a good actress," she stated.
"What?"
"I totally believed you when you said there was nothing going on between you and Oliver."
"There isn't."
Jess arched her eyebrow before pointing past me at

the dance floor.
"I saw you. Hell, the whole *room* saw you. You guys were grinding on each other like a cat up a scratching post."
I let out a laugh.
"Nice image."
"I'm not joking, Beccy," Jess said, leaning closer to me and glancing around the room. "Everyone's talking about you two."
I glanced around. A few people were looking at me, but they didn't look judge-y. I shrugged.
"Jess, I don't care. If people want to talk, they can. I finally know how I feel about Oliver and how he feels about me."
"Are you sure about that?"
"Yes," I said firmly, but inside I wavered a little. We hadn't actually said anything specific to each other. And I suppose we'd never really talked about the potential of us... I shook my hand dismissively.
"I mean it," I repeated in a firm tone. "Oliver and I are just friends and that's that."
I turned to the barman and ordered a drink. Tonight was my last night with him, and Jess, and there was no way I was going to spend it trying to live up to other people's expectations. Tonight was about having fun, with no labels, strings or anything else attached.
And fun we had. As the hours flashed by in a sparkly disco-ball kind of way, and I lost count of how many shots of alcohol I consumed, it all began to blur into a hazy mess of cuddles, dances and laughter. But I couldn't have wished for a better end to what had been one of the best experiences of my life. I'd made two new friends, who I hoped

with all my heart would remain in my life for years to come, I'd put in a promising and successful performance for the movie (I had that on good authority, that wasn't just me being big-headed) and I'd *survived.* There was an element of that, having been away from home for the first time. And by home, I meant the security of my life before, the support network I'd built around myself. I'd embraced the challenge and I'd succeeded. Although it was with a heavy heart that I checked in at the airport for my return flight to JFK two days later, there was a part of my soul that felt as if it had grown a few sizes.

MAY 5th

So it wasn't exactly the welcome home I'd been expecting…
After a two hour flight, and a half hour transfer from JFK, I slipped the key into my apartment door feeling excited. I hadn't seen Josh in such a long time, we had so much to catch up on. And now my Canadian adventure had come to an end, I realised I had kind of missed him.
"Hello?" I called, as I pushed the door open and heaved my suitcase inside. I put my heavy sports bag down beside it with a lumpy thump and shut the door. Hearing the distant noise of the TV, I headed quickly into the living area and saw Josh peering over the top of the sofa at me. But I came to a sliding halt when I saw another head beside him. A redhead.
Lori turned to look at me and I stared down at them in confusion, looking from face to face. What

an unusual guest, I thought. I didn't know they were friends.
"Hi," I smiled.
"Hey," she smiled back politely, before dropping her gaze and staring down into her lap. For some reason my eyes followed hers and came to rest on her hand, intertwined with Josh's, on her lap.
Oh...
My smile faded fast.
Josh jumped up and opened his arms, coming over and throwing them around me for our reunion hug. It didn't feel how I'd hoped it would.
"It's good to have you back," he said.
I looked up at him, my face unable to mask the painful realisation of the unexpected situation I'd just walked in on. He saw and looked embarrassed.
"Come with me," he said in a low whisper, before turning to look at Lori. "I'll be right back."
She nodded and stared ahead at the TV. She looked uncomfortable, which was a whole lot better than smug, I supposed. Josh and I walked into the kitchen, far enough away that we knew she couldn't hear us. I simply looked at him, demanding a proper explanation. Not that I didn't already know what was going on. But a tiny piece of me was hoping I was wrong.
"I didn't want you to find out this way," he stated.
"But you knew I was coming home today."
"I figured you'd take a later flight," he reasoned. "You hate getting up in the mornings."
It was a reasonable comment but it divided me. Half of me noted how sweet it was that he knew me so well. The other half felt mildly insulted. I simply shrugged in response, pushing my hair

behind my ears then folding my arms in front of me. I stared across the room towards where I knew she was sitting, all effortlessly gorgeous with her beautiful and striking red hair. I looked at Josh.
"I don't understand," I said quietly and honestly. "It's only been four weeks."
Josh nodded, looking awkward.
"But…" he said, daringly, "it *has* been six months since we broke up."
I had nothing to say to that.
"So how did this happen?"
"The usual way. We just started hanging out…"
I felt a stab of irrational jealousy. That was our thing, my head screamed, *we* hung out. How dare she? And on my sofa, in my apartment? But as I looked up at him, I realised I had no say in this. It was out of my hands. Josh was my ex-boyfriend and now he'd found someone new. But boy, did it hurt.
"How was the shoot?" Josh asked brightly, definitely trying to change the subject and lighten the mood.
I nodded, but my mind was in a daze.
"We'll go out if you want," Josh said, touching my arm. He looked so sincere. I took a deep breath and shook my head.
"No, it's okay. Really."
He didn't believe me but he didn't push it either.
"You want some help with your bags?" he asked.
"Actually, that'd be great, yeah."
Josh took the suitcase and I took the bag. I glanced awkwardly at Lori as we passed by to go up the stairs but she wasn't looking at me. I'd always liked her, actually. We got on fine. But she wasn't the

Lori who'd been a friend to me when I'd started seeing Riley, her co-star. It was like an evil twin had replaced her. She was dating Josh now… I could barely even form those words on my tongue without choking on them.
"So," Josh said, setting the bag down, "are you just going to be, like, unpacking and stuff?"
I looked around the bedroom. It seemed less welcoming than I thought it would. Suddenly I realised I didn't feel like I was home at all. More like I'd stepped into an alternate universe. I nodded vaguely.
"Okay, well, we'll be downstairs," Josh replied.
'We'. Ugh. And with that, he shut the door and I was alone. Again. I was so sick of being alone.
I called Steph, which turned out to be the best possible thing I could have done. She was surprised but talked rationally about it all, how it was unfair of me to expect him to be single forever and how it was a bonus that I actually knew Lori and she wasn't some horrible, bitchy stranger. Then she told me how she and Freddie had settled into their new place in LA, how close it was to the beach and that they were even considering getting a dog.
It was a happy, distracting sort of conversation that lasted the best part of an hour. But as soon as I hung up, it was back to the cold, lonely reality of my life.
I dared to venture downstairs, figuring hell, this was my apartment after all. But they were gone.
There was a note on the side in the kitchen: 'Gone out for lunch. Be back later'. I made myself some food then wandered into the living area. I stared down at the sofa, a hazy mirage of them cuddled

up holding hands blurring my real vision. That sofa was tainted now.
I sighed and sat down, scolding myself for being so immature. I turned on the TV and flicked aimlessly through the channels when I came across an old re-run of Hazy Days.
So that was a torturous experience I could have done without. It was like I was punishing myself, which made no sense - I'd already been hurt enough today. I didn't laugh at any of the jokes, even though it was that hilarious episode at the funfair. Instead I mourned the loss of my relationship with Riley and realised just how effortlessly gorgeous Lori was. When the credits rolled, I half expected a tear to roll down my cheek too. Instead, I muted the TV and sat in a sort of stunned silence.
The apartment was like a hollow shell of its former self. I'd had such amazing memories here, and it had always been so full of laughter and happiness. Now Steph was gone, Seth too, and all that remained was Josh, who'd invaded our space with another girl. His new girl.
I didn't want to be here anymore, I realised, and decided if I could control nothing else, then that was going to be my new mission. It was time to move out and move on. It hadn’t occurred to me that even after all this time, that perhaps I hadn't really moved on properly after breaking up with Josh. Well, that time had finally come. I was getting the hell out of that apartment.
But where was I going to go?

MAY 12th

"Happy birthday!" I chimed as the door swung open.
The beaming smile slid from my face.
"Oh," I said dejectedly. "It's you."
"Welcome home to you too, lil sis."
David smiled curiously at me and I shook my head with a smile.
"I figured the birthday girl would be answering the door is all. Sorry."
I stepped inside and hugged my big brother. As soon as I felt his arms around me, I felt safe. I loved having a big brother, even if I did hardly see him these days.
"You on your own?" he asked, peering behind me.
It was a casual statement but I felt a pang in my heart. It was a confirmation of my very single status, and that's what had hurt. I nodded in a bright but fake way as he shut the door.
"She's out back," David stated.

I wandered through the familiar hallway of my family home. It always felt good to come back here, to Philly. It was the place I knew I truly belonged, no matter how well my career, my relationships or just my life in general was going. I guess that's what being part of a family was all about - unconditional acceptance.
"So no boyfriend then?" David asked.
Oh, and some teasing banter, of course.
"Not at the moment."
"That's unlike you."
"Yeah it is…" I said, already tired of the dialogue.
"Where is she?"
I saw the white marquee in the garden just as the words left my mouth.
"Duh," David joked and I rolled my eyes at him.
"So getting older hasn't made you more mature then? That's a sad trade-off for those wrinkles…"
David reached up and touched his face in horror.
"I haven't…"
I couldn't hide my grin and he narrowed his eyes at me, launching himself at my middle and giving it a rough but ticklish squeeze. I batted him away with my free arm, trying not to drop the present I was carrying.
"Beccy!"
Vicky came rushing towards me, her pretty flowered sundress flapping behind her. I bent down and opened my arms as she flung hers around my neck.
"Hey!"
"I'm so happy to see you!" she grinned. "Come on! Stacey's opened nearly all her presents."
"Am I the last one here?" I asked.

"As usual," David mocked and I ignored him. Maybe it wasn't all that great having an older brother, after all… The three of us walked across the lawn and Vicky excitedly held back the door to the marquee for us.
"How old are you now? Thirteen? Fourteen?" I asked her teasingly.
"Ten, silly," she said, proudly puffing out her chest. I wide-eyed her before smoothing my hand down her dark brown hair, that was now just past her shoulders.
"You've definitely got bigger since I last saw you."
"You never come and see us anymore," she pouted, and I sighed, putting my arm around her and clasping her shoulder. I leant down and kissed her cheek.
"I'm sorry," I said. "I promise I'll make more of an effort, okay?"
I looked up and saw the rest of my family, sat around a long table covered in white linen and flowers. The banner behind Stacey, sitting at the head of the table, read 'Happy 21st Birthday'. I smiled. I really should make more of an effort to come home, I thought.
"Beccy!"
Joshua, the not-so-smallest-anymore, saw me first and gave me a wave but then every head turned to greet me. Mom and Dad. Ali. Sarah. Stacey. They were faces I knew and loved well and yet they all looked so different. Sarah's blonde hair was in a pretty bob now, and she looked every inch the awkward mid-teen that she now was, peeking out from behind her hair with a smile. Ali, just a year older, barely glanced at me before returning to his

Game Boy Advance. Mom gave me a warm smile and a wave, and I noticed she too had a new hairstyle, her blonde hair a wavy short bob that took years off her. Dad gave me a nod, unsurprisingly - he was a reserved kind of father, always there for us but in a subtle, serious kind of a way. And Stacey was getting up to come and see me. She was so glamorous, the blonde to my brunette, and I could see why she'd been so popular at school. Following in her footsteps had never been easy and I doubted it would ever change, no matter how old we were.
"Beccy, hey," she smiled, embracing me. I gave her a squeeze.
"Hey," I replied. " Happy birthday!"
She rolled her eyes and smiled.
"I can't believe I'm so old."
"You can do anything you want now you're 21," I countered. She smiled and I handed her my present. Her eyes lit up.
"Thanks, sis!"
She went back to the table and I went around gave everyone a hug and a kiss, even if they didn't want it (mostly the boys). Then I took a seat beside Vicky, who'd saved me one excitedly, and I watched as Stacey unwrapped my gift.
I knew it was perfect the moment I laid eyes on it. The brand new top-of-the-range camera achieved a series of 'ooh's and 'aah's' around the table and I grinned proudly.
"I know your other one was on the way out, and with the trip to Australia coming up..."
Stacey locked eyes with me and smiled.
"Thank you so much."

She continued to unwrap my other present, a spotty photo album the perfect accompaniment. Then she began unwrapping the camera itself, determined to start taking pictures right away. I looked around the table - whenever the whole Russo family was together, it was always an event that was worth capturing.
A loud 'whoop whoop' shattered the excited chatter and we turned to see Evan coming in, followed by Aunt Maddie.
"Apologies for my son," she said, rolling her eyes, as Evan strutted comically towards the table. I felt excited and patted the empty seat beside me. That was lucky. Stacey jumped up and ran around to greet them, then Evan came over towards me. I gave him a hug of my own as he gave Vicky a wave and nodded towards my parents.
"It's so good to see you, cuz," I beamed, as we sat down side by side. He leaned in.
"So now Stacey's 21 do you think…I mean…"
He looked around then reached for his empty glass.
"Is there going to be alcohol served at this thing?"
I giggled.
"Uh, no, I don't think it works like that."
He slammed his hand on the table, drawing the attention of Joshua, Ali and Sarah opposite.
"Damn," he cursed, before flashing me a grin.
My attention was distracted by the arrival of the food. Caterers were the obvious choice, being as there were eleven of us, and they came in carrying platters of tea-party food - sandwiches, macaroons, chips and dips, mini quiches. We watched as they were set down in the middle of the long table and my tummy began to rumble.

My Dad stood up and took a bottle of champagne from one of the waiters.
"If I can have everyone's attention, please."
His voice commanded us the same way it had done when we were kids and we all stopped talking and looked his way.
"I want to raise a toast to the birthday girl. Our big girl, who was once our first little girl..."
I looked at Stacey, who was smiling up at Dad.
"Your mother and I can't believe it's been 21 years since you first came into the world, a beautiful bundle of blonde curls and squishy cheeks."
I giggled at the unusual turn of phrase and so did Stacey, as she lowered her gaze bashfully.
"And now here you sit, as beautiful as ever, with the whole world at your feet. You always were the most charming girl in the room but now you're a woman...and you're as charming as ever."
"Oh Dan," my Mom said, batting her hand at him.
"Come on," he said, looking down at her as he held his hand in gesture at Stacey. "We have produced one beautiful daughter..."
I felt a pang of disappointment until he looked down the table and threw his arm wide.
"*Daughters*, I should say. And some handsome-looking sons too."
David pretended to adjust a bow-tie before slapping Ali on the back, who just slunk in his seat and hid behind his floppy hair.
"But kids, you know all that stuff, as wonderful as it is, means nothing in comparison to how proud we are of you all as individuals. You've made me and your Mom so, *so* proud, every single one of you."

My heart swelled inside my chest and I smiled around at my siblings, leaving the last smile for my Dad.
"And so, on Stacey's 21st, I'd like to thank our absentee children David and Beccy for coming home..."
David and I shared a smile before looking up at the table again.
"And to Maddie and Evan for sharing the occasion with us..."
I nudged Evan playfully and he nudged me back.
"And so without further ado, I'd like to wish Stacey a very Happy Birthday."
Dad held the champagne bottle and we winced, hunching our shoulders and waiting for the...
POP!
The cork flew off and we all cheered, as Dad filled Stacey's glass.
"Happy birthday!" Mom said, and we all chorused behind her, wishing Stacey well. Dad filled up the grown-up glasses and gave Evan a playful ruffle of his hair when he jokingly raised his glass. One of the waiters was following behind, filling everyone else's with orange juice.
"Why do I always feel like a kid when I come here?" Evan said, holding his glass up and staring at it disappointingly.
"I think we'll always feel like kids here," I mused, my mind filled with summers playing in the garden, spraying each other with water guns and playing hide and seek. We might have all grown up but we would always be family.
"To Stacey," my Dad announced.
"To Stacey!" we chorused, clinking glasses.

***

"So how's things going with you?" Evan asked, as we tucked into our food.
I sighed and looked at him, wearing a disenchanted expression.
"That good, huh?" he remarked. "What's happening with Riley?"
"We broke up months ago."
"Why?"
"Because he was jealous of my relationship with Josh."
Evan raised an eyebow, mid-bite of a mini-quiche.
"What? Are you two…"
"Ha! Far from it. He's started seeing Lori Palmer."
"Is she the girl from Hazy Days?"
I nodded, reaching for my drink.
"So how do you feel about that?" Evan enquired.
"Awful," I confessed. "And the worst part about it is, I'm not *allowed* to feel this way."
"What do you mean?"
"So what if Josh has a girlfriend? We're not together anymore. We haven't been in six months. And *I* broke up with *him*, for Riley, so it's not even like I can play that card either."
Evan nodded thoughtfully.
"Yeah, but it still sucks when someone you love moves on."
"Of course, I haven't even asked. How's things with you and Sadie?"
"Non-existent," Evan replied flatly.
"I'm sorry."
"Don't be. Hell, it's probably a lucky escape. She's a *nightmare*, you know that. I'd probably be miserable

if we were together…"
"But you're miserable now, right?"
Evan raised his eyes to look at me as I continued.
"And I'm guessing you're thinking you might as well be with her at least, if you're feeling that way."
Evan paused then nodded. He was always able to be honest with me. He sighed, pushing his fingers through his blonde floppy fringe, which fell straight back over his eyes when he lowered his hand again.
"I don't know, Beccy. I want to move on. I want to date other people. It's just…I can't forget about her. She's like the benchmark now, that all other girls are judged by. And you know Sadie - she's one of a kind."
I nodded and smiled. Sadie could be a handful, sure, and she was unrelentingly self-absorbed and spoilt. And she never stopped talking…loudly, for that matter. But she had a heart of gold and to know her was to love her. Unconditionally. I gave Evan a gentle nudge.
"You'll find someone."
"So will you."
I nodded and took a sip of my drink.
"So what's happening now that Josh has a girlfriend? I thought you guys were living together," Evan remarked.
"We are."
"Will you move in with Steph?"
I jerked my head back and stared at him.
"What?" he asked.
"She's moved to LA."
"Since when? With who?"
I filled him in on the break-up with Seth, and the

very quick make-up with Freddie, and how they'd both moved out, leaving just Josh and I behind.
"We're barely covering the rent," I confessed, "especially with the Lexington apartment too."
Evan reached for a baby blue macaroon and took a bite, smiling a contented smile as he brushed the crumbs from his lip.
"Hey," he said, quirking an eyebrow, "I just had a thought."
"Go on. I know how rare they are."
He mock-gasped and I giggled.
"What would you say to you moving out…"
"It's inevitable now, I think. It makes no sense to have that apartment with Josh, especially now…"
"With me?"
I stopped rambling and looked Evan straight in the eyes. He was serious. Now *that* was rare.
"Really?"
He nodded.
"I've been thinking of moving out this year but I didn't want to do it alone."
"Aww..."
He rolled his eyes.
"Not because I'm scared or anything," he said, tugging at his t-shirt. "I just…"
I smiled, patting his arm.
"I'm teasing you. Moving out on your own doesn't make any sense."
"But moving in with you does."
I stared up at the roof of the marquee.
"Think about it," he said. "We get along great…"
"That's an over-statement," I teased, and we shared a smile.
" See!" he beamed. "And you're looking for

somewhere to move to..."
"What, here? I can't live in Philly. It's too far from Lexington."
"No, I could come to New York...we could live in the suburbs!" he said, the excitement rising in his voice. "We could be living the regular suburban dream!"
I giggled then let my mind wander to what it really would be like to live with Evan. I couldn't think of a single reason not to. I turned and looked at him, a wild excited grin spreading across my face.
"Are we really going to do this?"
"I'm game if you are," he grinned back.
I squealed and threw my arms around his neck, giving him a squeeze.
"What the...?" David asked.
"What's going on down there?" Mom called. Evan and I looked at each other, our arms still around each other, then looked around the table.
"We're moving in together!"
I looked at Evan, smiling back at me, and realised he was my knight in shining armour. He'd solved all my problems in one afternoon. Maybe he would restore my faith in the opposite sex after all.

JUNE 2nd

Once Evan and I had taken some time to really consider the proposition of moving in together, it was full steam ahead with finding a place and signing on that dotted line. After suggesting the suburbs, I found myself drawn to the idea of a little house somewhere in a quiet street, away from the bright lights of the big city. I'd done that, and I'd loved it, but I wanted this to be a different experience.

We found an adorable little three-bed house in Pleasant Plains, Staten Island, and we fell in love with it. It was grown up in its own way but small enough for two relatively-new-at-being-old kids to cope with. We signed the lease (for a year) and that was that.

But then came telling Josh. I'd decided I wasn't going to mention it to him until everything was finalised. And besides, I hadn't seen him much. He and Lori were most definitely in some sort of honeymoon period, which thankfully, they'd done mostly out of sight or at her parent's place uptown. Of course we'd been together on set, but we'd fallen back into a productive working kind of relationship, which I think we'd both done to avoid talking about how much things had changed between us in a relatively short amount of time. But over breakfast one morning in Lexington, with the big move just days away, time had run out for my confession.

"I've been meaning to talk to you, actually," I said, trying to sound breezy, but the words themselves were tinged with seriousness. Josh handed me a cup of coffee and sort of held it there between us.

"Oh really?"

I took it from him, our eyes locked together, but I tore them away and wandered over towards the couch. I hovered behind it then turned and sat leaning against the back.

"I, uh...I'm moving out."

Josh looked at me.

"You're what?"

"I'm moving out. Of the New York apartment."

He frowned.

"When?"

"Uh...Wednesday."

His eyebrow arched sharply.

"*This* Wednesday?" he said, folding his arms. "And you're telling me this now? Where are you going?"

"Staten Island. This little place called Pleasant Plains."

Josh nodded slowly. Then he cleared his throat.

"And with who?"

"Evan."
I visibly saw the relief spread across his face. It wasn't Riley. It wasn't some new guy I hadn't mentioned. It was Evan, my cousin. He could deal with that. But he still looked disappointed as he reached for his coffee and came towards me, hovering close by.
"I don't understand why you kept it secret."
"I just..." I shrugged, "I figured with all your stuff going on..."
"If by 'stuff' you mean Lori, then..."
He didn't know quite what to say. He ran his hand through his hair and sighed.
"I really messed this up, didn't I?"
I looked up at him.
"Yeah, you kind of did," I said gently. "Coming back to that wasn't exactly the highlight of my year so far."
He nodded.
"You didn't mention it when we talked," I continued. "You gave me absolutely no clue that anything was going on..."
"I didn't know what to say," he shrugged apologetically and I nodded.
"You should have been honest with me."
Josh paused and looked at me.
"I'm sorry."
I nodded at him. There wasn't much more to say than that.
"So you're leaving because you feel uncomfortable?" he asked.
I didn't want that to be the only reason, though it was one of the main ones, so I shook my head.
"It's not that, not really. I hardly even see you two."

"We've been trying to keep our distance," he explained, with a hint of a smile.
"You know it's been tough making the rent since Steph and Seth moved out. And after doing Irresponsible Actions and coming back…I don't know. I feel like it's the end of an era."
Josh pouted, raising his eyebrows a little, and I smiled, rolling my eyes.
"Okay, that sounds dramatic. But I do feel like things have sort of run their course now, especially with that place. It's not what it used to be."
Josh nodded and came towards me, turning and sitting beside me.
"I know what you mean. It feels…"
"Empty?"
Josh nodded in agreement, taking a sip of his coffee. I watched him. He was still Josh, but things hadn't just changed between us. He'd changed too. He was letting his facial hair grow in a little (for her? Did she like that?) and his hair was a little longer, a little scruffier. We'd been working alongside each other for a few weeks now but that's all it had been. We were back to being co-stars and roommates, but it didn't feel right. We'd never been that before, we'd never meant so little to each other. It was like all we'd sought out in each other was being fulfilled by other people now, through other relationships. It hit me like a freight train - did we really need each other anymore?
"Maybe it's for the best," Josh mused, looking ahead towards the kitchen before turning his head to look at me.
"I mean, we've all got to move on sometime, right?"
When he put it like that…something inside my

heart died a little.

***

But then the big move was upon me, and my life became all about Evan. And boxes. Lots and lots of boxes. Josh had helped me pack up a few things and it had actually been kind of fun. Until that last moment when we stood and looked around the apartment together. Josh put his arm around me and I put my arm around him. I nestled into his shoulder and he kissed my forehead.
"It's been fun," he declared.
"But the fun isn't over yet…is it?" I asked, peering up at him. He looked down at me and the whole world seemed to fade away.
"It doesn't have to be," he said in such a way that I wondered just how strongly he could possibly feel about Lori if he was able to say such things, with such heartfelt sincerity, to me.
As I unpacked the boxes the other end, I came across all kinds of mementoes and keepsakes that reminded me of a life spent with Josh. Photographs and jewellery, even clothes I remembered wearing on dates together.
"You okay?" Evan had asked, as I stood staring at a shelving unit in the midst of a full-on daydream.
"Sure," I nodded, pushing all my distracting thoughts aside.
"You're not having second thoughts, are you?"
I turned and looked at Evan. I smiled and strode over to him, grabbing hold of him by the arms.
"No. I can't wait to see what the next chapter of my life has in store for me."

Evan grinned back.
"I'm thinking late night parties, all-night movie marathons..."
I raised my hand and he slapped his hard against it for a high five.
"Sounds good to me!" I chimed.

***

Later that night, on our first night in our new house, in my new bed, I was sending out texts about the move to almost everyone in my phone book until I'd come to Riley. Then I'd stopped.
I really missed him. As much as I still had feelings for Josh, Riley was the one I really craved being with again. Things between us had barely got going and then they were over. And now I was no longer living with Josh (the Lexington apartment, surely, was next to go), the one obstacle that was preventing us from being together was gone. It was with a feeling of rebellious nervousness that I sent a message to Riley, a relationship SOS. Nothing ventured, nothing gained, right?
Hi, it's Beccy. Just wanted to let you know I've moved in with my cousin Evan in Staten Island. Thinking of having a housewarming party in a few weeks. Maybe you could come... It would be great to see you. x
To my surprise, and complete excitement, he replied almost immediately.
That sounds great. Would love to see the new place...and you too, of course. Riley.
Heart pounding hard, I rushed into Evan's room to tell him.
"Sounds promising," he nodded, before raising an

eyebrow. "But since when are we having a housewarming party?"
Oops. I'd forgotten to mention that...

JUNE 22nd

I kicked the door gently with my foot and it swung open. I stepped inside, my arms loaded with paper bags full of party food, and yelled out,
"I'm ba-ack!"
I put the bags down on the side, my handbag too, then went over to close the door behind me. Evan came into the kitchen rubbing his hair dry with a towel. He was wearing a pair of jeans and a grey vest, which I assumed was halfway towards this evening's outfit.
"Did you manage to get everything?" he asked, and I peered inside the bags, rummaging around.
"Plates, cups, napkins, all the usual stuff. Plus I got another two bottles of soda and some more chips."
"You can never have enough chips," Evan agreed.
"What *is* the time...?" I mused, looking up at the kitchen clock. 4:55pm. I turned to Evan.
"Can you unpack this stuff and…"

He nodded, gently stepping into my space and pushing me out of the way as he reached into the bag.
"Go, go. We both know you want at least two hours to prep for Mr Kitson."
I flashed him a look but he was oblivious, already laying out various party requirements on the kitchen counter. So I turned and walked away, heading upstairs to my bedroom. Two hours was a little excessive but Evan wasn't wrong - I was definitely thinking about Riley and hoping he would show. There was no reason he wouldn't, of course, but that didn't stop me worrying. Or running through scenarios and conversation starters in my head. Or planning my final outfit right down to the earrings in my ears and the rings on my fingers. Tonight had a lot riding on it. So I went straight into the en-suite and turned on the shower. The guests were due from six o' clock so Operation Attraction was right on schedule...

***

When I finally made it back downstairs to the kitchen, I was blowing on my still-sticky fingernails and wishing I'd painted them the day before. *Stupid...*
"How's it going?" I asked, as Evan stood checking his phone.
"All done."
"Really?" I asked, looking around. There were stacks of cups on the side, next to rows of unopened bottles of juice and soda (and a few sneaky beers). The chips were in brightly coloured

bowls and I could smell the pizza that was cooking in the oven. I nodded and folded my arms across my pretty flowered sundress. I'd opted to go barefoot - it was a house party, after all.
"I'm impressed," I complimented.
Evan shrugged casually, as if it was no big deal that he'd single-handedly prepared for a party, and done it all on time too. But I was impressed - this was a guy who had always, *always* been late for high school and never, *ever* remembered to bring a pen to class. Maybe we really were growing up.
"Who are you texting?" I asked, coming to stand by the counter and reaching for a chip. As I put it in my mouth and crunched, he looked up.
"Oh, no one... Shall I put the music on?"
"Good idea," I nodded, looking around. "The only thing this place is lacking is atmosphere."
"And people," he said, as he brushed past.
"And that, too."
As if on cue, the doorbell rang. Evan stopped and looked at me, and I at him. We both wide-eyed each other and grinned.
"Well, go on then!" he said, gesturing at the door. "Let them in."
I skipped over to the door and flung it open.
"Hey!" Jenna grinned, her smile stretched wide across her face and her arms open too.
"Come in!" I said, stepping back and holding the door. She came inside and pushed her sunglasses on top of her head, looking all around at the kitchen.
"So you found us alright?"
"Oh yeah," she nodded, her eyes distracted as she had a good look around.

"You're first here," I told her and she nodded, before looking at me and smiling.
"Well, I am the closest now..."
"Of course!"
"I'm right around the corner, actually. Near Princes Bay."
"On the seafront?"
She nodded again, beaming with pride. Evan came in and raised his hand.
"Hey Jenna."
"Hey Evan," she said, and they walked towards each other before embracing, just as the doorbell rang again. I went over and opened the door, pausing before grinning from ear to ear.
"Hey gorgeous."
Oliver smiled at me, that deep and sexy British accent music to my ears. I suddenly felt excited to see him again and followed this feeling by throwing my arms around him and giving him a tight squeeze.
"Thank you so much for coming!" I said, stepping back and holding open the door.
"My pleasure," he charmed, peering around the door.
"Guys!" I called. "This is Oliver."
"Hi," Jenna waved, as Evan raised his hand in acknowledgement.
"Come on in," he said, so Oliver took a hesitant few steps inside as I closed the door behind him.
"You got here okay, then?" I asked brightly.
Oliver turned and looked at me and I got a moment to drink in those beautiful dark curls, his warm, smiling eyes and that unmistakeable aura of confidence that he so effortlessly exuded.

"It's amazing how postcodes work, isn't it? You just give one to the taxi driver and then they magically find the place..."
I tipped my head to the side and arched my eyebrow.
"You mean zip codes and cab drivers..."
Oliver smirked and raised his finger, giving me a nod.
"Yes, I do."
I smiled and gestured towards the drinks.
"Can I get you something? A beer?"
"Sure," he said, following me over. Evan had even laid out a bottle opener on the side - how organised - and I cracked the cap off before handing Oliver the bottle.
"To your new place," he toasted, and I quickly poured myself a cup of orange juice before raising it towards him.
"To my new place."
We both took a sip then I nodded at him, catching his eye.
"So how's things going? What are you doing at the moment?"
"Not much. I've got some downtime between projects so I'm staying with a friend from the Crusader movies, Dylan Merryman..."
An image of the guy, one of Oliver's co-stars, popped into my head. I knew of him, but I didn't know him personally. The doorbell rang again and both of us looked over.
"Come with me," I said, as Evan went towards the door. "Let me introduce you to my friend Jenna."
Oliver followed and Jenna watched, smiling her most charming of smiles.

"Hi," she said, holding out her hand. "I'm Jenna."
"Oliver," he said, taking her hand and pulling her close, kissing her on one cheek then the other.
Jenna held her hand to her chest.
"What manners."
Oliver flashed me a smile and I knew they would hit it off, so I let my eyes wander over to the door, where Stacey was giving me a hearty wave, her boyfriend Ben just behind her.

***

The next half an hour or so went by in a blur of hugs, kisses and handshakes. I tried my best to introduce people and make connections but to be honest, I acted more like a doorman, opening and closing the door and directing people to drinks. But as the place began to fill up (no matter how many times I encouraged people to head through into the living room, everyone stayed squashed up in the kitchen), there was one notable absence.
I was just filling Jess in on what I'd been up to since I'd got back when the doorbell rang.
"Excuse me," I said, making my way over. I was on auto-pilot and wasn't really thinking about who might be on the other side when I opened it and looked out. It was Riley.
He was standing on the doorstep, looking over his shoulder. Wearing a deep blue checked shirt, sleeves rolled up, his hands were casually pushed into the pockets of his jeans. He turned to look at me, his floppy hair casually flicking as he did so, and locked his eyes on me. Those dark chocolate brown eyes. And there was the smirk, the one that

hid naughty intentions I was secretly pleased he still had for me.
"Hey butterfly."
My heart nearly imploded.
"Hi," I smiled, unable to keep a cool, calm exterior. I was almost certainly grinning like a Cheshire cat.
"Come in," I welcomed, holding open the door. He stepped past me and I breathed him in. The familiarity of his scent brought back memories of cuddles and kisses and our bodies being pressed together. I was brought back to Earth with a bump when I heard my name called from up the driveway and knew exactly who it was - Josh.
Riley stopped and I wanted to hurry him inside but there was no time. Josh was at the doorstep and they were face to face again for the first time since New Year's Eve.
The usually happy and warm expression that Josh carried was replaced with a stern and serious face of recognition. Behind him came Lori, who saw me and looked awkward, but then saw Riley and looked pleased. They were friends at least in this excruciatingly uncomfortable love square.
"Hi," I said, stepping into the space between the boys that seemed to be crackling with tension.
Josh, whose gaze was broken, finally saw me, properly, and smiled.
"Hey."
"Hi Lori," I said brightly, trying a new and accepting 'me' on for size. She smiled back politely and nodded, looking up towards the roof.
"You have a lovely house."
"Thank you," I replied, stepping back. "Come on in."

Riley, to my relief, had decided to go and blend in with the crowd and Josh and Lori, who were now holding hands (duly noted), came inside.
"It's big," Josh noted, and I nodded.
"Yeah, we really lucked out. And this is a great neighbourhood too, real friendly."
Josh nodded, his eyes drinking in his surroundings, then he turned and looked at Lori and gave her hand a gentle tug.
"Do you want a drink?"
"Sure," she smiled, just for him. I watched them, envious and jealous of this connection they had now. I felt like she'd just swooped in on him the moment I was out of the country and dug her claws in real good. And yet, there was another part of me that remembered I had liked her once, and that part was trying to convince the other part that she wasn't the backstabbing bitch I was trying to make her out to be. She was just smart and she'd seen that Josh was one of the good ones. I could hardly blame her for that.
I hadn't even really wanted to invite them. But once I'd spoken to Connor and Meghan and Jared about it, the news had spread quickly and Josh had cornered me on set.
"So what's this I hear you're having a housewarming party?"
It had caught me completely off guard. He knew this, but pretended he didn't.
"I take it my invite got lost in the post…"
I smiled and shook my head, covering my tracks.
"Of course not, silly. I just hadn't gotten around to speaking to you about it yet."
Both of us knew I was lying.

"And, uh…can I bring my plus one?" he asked tentatively.
In some ways, it had been even more of an affectionate nickname than if he'd called her 'sweetie' or 'honey' or even just Lori. 'Plus one'. My blood had boiled.
"Sure," I'd smiled through gritted teeth, thinking 'Of course I want my ex and his new girlfriend round to my house, abso-frickin-lutely!'.
And now he was here, and so was she, and so was…where *was* Riley? I turned and began to look for him. Stacey and Ben were chatting to Meghan, Jared was catching up with Jo Levine, and Oliver and Jenna looked like they were having a cosy chat on the sofa (mental note to keep an eye on those two…), but no sign of Riley.
Suddenly, a pair of strong arms wrapped themselves around me and picked me up off the floor. I shrieked and people close by looked as Riley set me down again. I grinned as I turned to face him and gave him a playful shove. He just looked into my eyes and made me feel like no time had passed between us, that nothing had changed.
"So where's your bedroom?" he smirked, leaning closer to me.
I gasped then decided to play along. First attack of Operation Attraction - out-and-out flirting.
"Upstairs, of course. Where bedrooms usually are," I replied.
"Is it big?"
I shrugged casually.
"I guess."
"And does it have…" he said, looking up at the ceiling and biting his lip in the sexiest of ways, "a

bed?"
"Well, I'm not sleeping on the floor," I replied curtly.
"Are you sleeping *alone*?" he asked, locking eyes with me. It took every ounce of self-control to keep calm.
"Evan and I are a little old for bunk beds," I remarked casually.
Riley went to smile then tried to hide it, but I saw. He nodded to himself, crossing his arms as he held onto his beer.
"That's a very good point..."
Strike one to me. Now it was *my* turn to smile.

***

The party was in full swing when I saw Riley next. I'd lost him in the crowd and had ended up drifting towards Oliver and Jenna.
"Where's the bathroom?" she asked me, and I gave her directions. As she left, Oliver raised his empty bottle and peered inside, then motioned to get up.
"No, stay there," I said,."I'll get you one."
"It's okay," he said, rising up. "I can't stay here all night."
We went into the kitchen and I got myself some more soda and grabbed a handful of chips. I glanced around and saw that a few of the bowls were empty so, courteous hostess that I am, I grabbed a bag and went around refilling them. But as I went to return, I saw Riley standing with Oliver so I hung back and watched. Deep in conversation, I noted just how beautiful they both were. Riley was sexier, more rugged, but Oliver

had such a pretty face... Damn. It was like a hot hunk face-off right in the middle of my kitchen. I took a few steps closer and realised I could hear them. And they hadn't noticed me. *Jackpot.*
"Yeah, she's a sweetheart," Oliver said.
"So you guys, you uh, you hit it off then?" Riley asked.
"Absolutely. Which was such a relief because you just don't know with co-stars if you're even going to *like* each other, which makes the job that much harder, doesn't it?"
"Sure," Riley nodded, glancing at his beer before taking a sip."But you two liked each other?"
"Oh yes, I like her a lot. She's a lovely girl. We had a lot of fun together. She's, hmmm...how can I describe her?"
Oliver paused and Riley just stared, waiting with anticipation. Then Oliver let out a gentle laugh.
"Spirited. Yes, Beccy is what I'd called 'spirited'."
"*Spirited*?" Riley asked, his eyebrow quirked. He clearly didn't know quite what to read into that. But before he could ask any more probing questions, he'd spotted me and I had to pretend like I hadn't been an eavesdropping fly-on-the-wall. I came up beside Oliver, who grinned and threw his arm around my shoulder, pulling me into him and kissing my cheek.
"And here she is!" he grinned. "We've just been talking about you."
Showing just what an honest guy he was, I was impressed he had decided to reveal all to me.
"Oh you were?" I played along, giving Riley a smile. He was watching us as closely as I'd been watching Josh and Lori. But he raised his guard

almost immediately, giving me a carefree shrug and taking a swig of his beer.
"Should you be drinking that?" I asked with a smirk. I raised my finger and gave it a wag. Riley looked me right in the eyes, flashing me a sexy smile.
"You know I don't like playing by the rules."
Strike two to Riley - I'd come over a little light-headed after that audio-visual combination.
"Right," Oliver said, and we both looked at him.
"It's time you and I had a little dance. Come on."
He took my hand and pulled me away from Riley, which neither of us were very keen on. I gave him a longing look as Oliver gave me one final tug out of sight, leading me towards the living room. He pushed the coffee table to one side and it slid across the rug.
"I didn't know you were into interior design," I remarked, hands on my hips.
"This place is lacking a dance floor," he said smartly, "and I intend on rectifying that."
"Hell yeah!" Jenna said, coming towards me and taking my hand. I tuned into the song that was playing - 'Hot In Herre' - and grinned. Perfect.
"Let's crank it up!" Evan said, spinning the dial so the music burst from the speakers, the bassline thudding through the floor.
"We have neighbours!" I called back at him and he grinned, shimmying towards me.
"Then let's introduce ourselves to them, shall we?" he called back and I glared at him before grinning, as he twirled me under his arm. I turned towards Oliver and we began to dance like we had at the after-party, getting lost in the moment and the

comfortable way he made me feel, even when we were bumping and grinding on each other. The scene was set, the music was perfect, but the side glances and sniggers from Evan and Jenna reminded me that this wasn't my usual behaviour. I just seemed to forget myself around Oliver, and I certainly seemed to forget my inhibitions.
Trying to move away, Oliver grinned and pulled me right back in, our bodies bumping together.
"Don't think you're getting away from me that easily," he charmed and I giggled, deciding to hell with it - this was my party, my house, and my rules. I didn't care what anyone else thought. Until I saw Riley loitering in the corner, looking very isolated and disapproving. I wasn't exactly giving off the right signals to him and despite whatever I had going on with Oliver, what I wanted to have again with Riley had to be my priority. And besides, I knew Oliver would understand. We'd discussed 'The Riley Situation' a lot when we'd been in Montreal.
"We've got a bit of an audience," I called into his ear.
"Can't help that," Oliver shrugged with a grin. "People enjoy looking at beautiful things."
I laughed and shook my head, leaning in again, my hands on his shoulders, his on my waist.
"No, it's Riley. I think he's jealous."
Oliver leaned his head back and arched his eyebrow.
"Shall we make him really jealous?"
"*No...*" I said, as he grabbed hold of me and tipped me back, nuzzling his face into my neck as I clung to him. I protested and wriggled until he finally

righted me and I glared at him, only half seriously of course.
"Go on," he said, thumbing over his shoulder. "Ditch me for your man."
"It's not like that."
"I know," he smiled. "I'm just joking with you. But..."
He stepped closer and put his hand on my arm, looking into my eyes. I looked back, seeing a more serious side to my playful playmate for perhaps the first time ever.
"You make sure he knows how lucky he is to have a second chance with you, okay?"
I nodded. Oliver looked a little harder, a little deeper into my eyes, then nodded too.
"Now get out of here," he said, leaning around to slap me on the butt. I jumped forwards and yelped, turning to give him a slap on the arm, before looking towards Riley. He was gone.
I hurried into the kitchen and scanned the room for his blue checked shirt. He was at least a head above everyone else so why couldn't I see him? What I did see was the door closing...
I raced over to it and pulled it open, hurrying outside, and there he was.
"Riley, wait! Don't go!" I called out in a panic.
He turned towards me, a cigarette between his lips and a lighter in his hand. He wasn't leaving - he was going for a smoke. *Cringe*. He smiled, knowing I'd let my guard down. Strike three to Riley, and I was out.
I walked towards him with purposeful and slow steps, clasping my hands behind my back.
"So I might have just embarrassed myself a little..."

I said, looking up at him and holding apart my forefinger and thumb in gesture. Riley inhaled and put his lighter into his back pocket, breathing out a cloud of smoke and nodding, running his other hand through his hair.
"Just a little," he said, mimicking my gesture with his thumb and forefinger. I pushed his hand down between us and realised I was standing very close to him. And yet somehow, it didn't seem close enough. I gazed up at him, the dark sky behind his head and the security light illuminating his handsome features. He reached up and pushed a strand of my hair behind my ear, his fingertips gently brushing my cheek as my skin tingled at his touch.
Riley looked into my eyes, narrowing his own slightly, as if he was trying to figure me out.
"Oliver and I, we're just friends," I said, trying to help him out a little. He nodded.
"He likes you," he said. "He told me."
"And I like him," I said, nodding, before looking back up and forcing myself to keep eye contact, no matter how intense.
"But that's all."
Riley looked at me, searching my eyes for the truth. Seeming to find it, he smiled slowly, seductively.
"Are you trying to tell me something?" he purred.
I smiled, feeling my cheeks warming, reddening, as I blushed.
"I might be…" I replied, dropping my gaze. He reached up and placed his finger under my chin, before leaning close to my ear and whispering, his breath warm on my neck,
"Consider the message received."

He lingered for just a moment, his finger under my chin, his face hovering beside mine, letting the heat between us intensify. Then he let go, stepped back a little and took another cool and nonchalant drag on his cigarette. I was putty in his hand.
"So Josh and Lori?" he said, looking up at the stars. "I didn't see that one coming."
"No, me either. I came back from Montreal and quite literally walked in on them."
He snapped his head to look at me and I knew which dots he'd connected.
"Oh no," I said, waving my hand dismissively. "Not like that. God, no..."
"That would have been a bit awkward."
"Oh God, like...*horrible.*"
Riley looked at me.
"You and him...what's the status between you two now?"
I looked up at him. This was a serious question.
"We're friends. Obviously we're not living together anymore, and he's with Lori, so... I guess that's all we are now."
"You don't sound that sure," he commented. "Or that happy."
I shrugged.
"You know first-hand how complicated the dynamic is between Josh and I..."
With a roll of the eyes, Riley acknowledged I was right.
"So I guess it's just a little strange for me for things to be so neatly compartmentalised. You know, this is it. This is what we are and that's it. Just like everyone else. Because, I don't know, it always felt more..."

"Special?" Riley offered and I nodded. Then I sighed.
"It doesn't matter," I said. "We don’t need to be talking about this."
"For what it's worth," Riley said, taking another drag before exhaling, "you guys definitely do have something special."
I looked at Riley, totally stunned. What a sweet and selfless thing to say about a relationship he didn't exactly rate very highly. He looked around, everywhere but at me, then finally, when I said and did nothing, his eyes came to rest on me.
"Well, who's to say that we won't have that someday too?" I offered, with an honest kind of hope in my voice. Riley looked back before smiling - not a smirk, but a sweet, genuine smile.
"That's a very good point."

***

Back inside the party, I ended up getting distracted and once again, we found ourselves on opposite sides of the room. Only this time when we caught each other's eyes, we'd smile a secret smile at each other, engaged in more of a long-distance kind of exercise. But I had him well and truly set in my sights…
The party was a great success, so much so that it ended up going on several hours longer than what was on the invite. But, one by one, two by two, people began to make their excuses and say their goodbyes until there was only Jenna, Oliver and Riley left. The other two awkwardly began to busy themselves with tidying up as Riley and I made our

way towards the door.
"So," he said, turning to face me and holding onto the edge of the door, "I haven't actually had a tour yet."
"Maybe next time," I smiled.
"So there's going to be a next time?"
I smiled and shrugged.
"It can be arranged."
Riley's smirk softened into smile.
"I'd like that."
"Me too."
With a quick glance over my shoulder to check no one was watching, he slid his hand onto my waist and brought his face close to mine. I closed my eyes, bracing myself for impact, but to my surprise, I felt his lips press against my cheek, not my lips. I opened my eyes again, clearly unable to mask my disappointment, because Riley's smirk was back.
"You should never let your opponent see your hand, Beccy. That's rule one."
Deciding I had no choice but to try to salvage this awkward and cringeworthy situation, I looked up into his eyes and said,
"I thought you told me you don't play by the rules."
"I do when there are hearts involved."
And so he left me standing at the door, with that curious remark and unkissed lips, as he disappeared into the night. Riley had definitely won the battle, but I was more determined than ever to win the war.

JULY 1st

So things have been slowly getting back to normal. Or should I say, a new kind of normal.
When I'm in Lexington, I've been choosing to spend a lot more time at Meghan's apartment than at my own, on account of Josh and Lori's developing relationship. The bed Josh and I used to share is now filled with someone else, and me playing third wheel on the sofa hasn't exactly been ideal for any one of us. So Meghan eventually asked me if I wanted to move in with her instead. She only has one room, so that would still mean me taking the sofa-bed in her lounge, but until I can find a new place of my own to rent (which is hardly worth doing until we come back for season four in the Fall) it actually seemed quite appealing. But try explaining that to Josh.
"I'm starting to get the impression that you really don't like me," he'd said when I told him I was

considering moving out. Again.
"Not at all."
He'd looked at me with one eyebrow raised and held my gaze until I'd crumbled.
"It's not that I don't like you, Josh. That will never be the case. It's just I feel like…well, I feel like I don't really know you anymore."
In my head that had sounded a little less harsh. Josh positively flinched.
"Do you really feel that way?"
"It's just, things have changed between us. You've moved on now, and so have I, and…"
"I thought we said we'd always be in each other's lives, no matter what," Josh said with a frown on his face.
"I know…"
"And that we didn't want to lose each other."
"I don't…"
"But you're going the right way about it, Beccy. You're severing all ties with me."
"I am not," I argued, but I couldn't really justify my actions in any other way. I was pulling away from him.
"We've got two weeks left of filming and then what? Will I even see you this summer?" Josh asked, searching my face for a yes. I could only give him a non-committal shrug.
So I'm in the process of trying to pack up all the things from the Lexington apartment and putting some of it in storage, ready for my next new place. Thankfully my other place is settled now, the house with Evan in Pleasant Plains. Although we only see each other once or twice a week at the most, we always try to make the most of it. We take it in

turns to choose a movie (he's never pleased when it's my choice, although I caught him getting teary-eyed over A Walk To Remember the other night) and we snuggle up on the sofa under our big cosy blanket and just hang out. Life sure is simple with Evan as my male companion. No drama, no second-guessing, no mind games.

That is definitely Riley's domain. Since the house-warming party we've been texting each other. *A lot.* Well, I say a lot, although we seem to go for days without a word, then we'll spend a whole evening sending messages back and forth. We're flirting, for sure, but it's not really going anywhere. Though that might all change if we end up going on this road trip together…

I finally heard from Steph after what seems like a lifetime. Apart from the occasional catching-up email, she's really fallen off the face of the planet. She's as loved up with Freddie as ever and enjoying the LA sunshine. But she got in touch to see if I fancied going on a road trip with her and Freddie through some of the North Eastern states. I'd never been on a road trip before and it had always been something that appealed to me, just hitting the road with friends and seeing the world. Steph was starting work on a horror movie in August so we didn't have much of a window between season finales on our shows and summer work (I was hitting the promotional trail for Irresponsible Actions in September too), but we were determined to make it happen.

I'd excitedly told Riley about our plans, to which he'd texted,

Sounds like fun. Can I come?

I didn't really even know if he was serious. If he wasn't, and I went down the route of asking him along, that would make me look a little too desperate for my liking. But if he was, and I dismissed him, what a wasted opportunity for a little make-or-break vacation together!

You're more than welcome had been my final reply, once I'd been brave enough to press send. That happened to be quite late at night, and the texting had stopped after that, so I'd fallen asleep. I woke up the next day panicking. Had I gone too far? Had I made myself look too keen? I didn't even feel like I could pull things back by joking it off because if he wasn't worrying about it, then he really would start to think I was crazy if I brought it up again. So I waited. For what seemed like forever. Eventually, a whole 24 hours later, he replied,

So what should I pack?

I'm still not sure if he's joking or not. But I have to find out because Steph's booking everything up soon and I need to get my head in the right place if I'm going to be holed up in a camper van with Riley Kitson for a week. What an intriguing prospect...

JULY 19th

So it turns out Riley *was* serious. Within days, the plans were set into motion (thanks to a very organised and motivated Stephanie Hunt) and it became all I could talk/think/dream about for the last few days of filming. When Josh found out how I planned to spend my summer vacation, he wished me the best of luck with an awkward pat on the back and that was that. Because Casey and Jonny have split up in the show, our final few scenes weren't even together and whatever reason we had left to see each other was gone. I saw him briefly at the wrap party and we shared a 'well done for surviving season three' hug but I'm starting to feel more estranged from him than ever. But we both seem happy, in our own very separate ways, so that's surely a good thing, really. At least that's what I keep telling myself.
But I haven't really had much time to think about

all that because I've been packing. I had circled the date, July 19th, on my calendar with a big, red circle and every day, it had thrilled me to realise I was getting ever closer to the big day. But this morning, I put a red cross through it because it was finally here.
Steph and Freddie arrived early this morning and pulled up outside the house with a big, loud toot of the horn. Evan was excited to see them and to show them around the house, which we did, before he helped me to the van with all my stuff. So it's not really a van, it's more of a motorhome. The living and sleeping areas are out back, like a trailer really, except it has the driver's cab at the front.
"I'm really going to miss you, cuz," Evan had said, throwing his arms around me and giving me a tight squeeze.
"I'll be back before you know it."
"You be careful," he warned, waving his finger at me with a serious expression.
"Yes, sir," I saluted, before cracking into a smile.
"I mean, be *careful*. I know you're going to turn this motorhome into your own private passion wagon, but that doesn't mean you have to be completely reckless."
"Evan! Gross..." I said, glaring at him as I gave him a playful shove. He grinned and backed himself up onto the sidewalk.
A yellow taxi came to a stop just in front of the motorhome and my heart began to race.
"And as if on cue..." Evan teased.
I flashed him a 'cut it out' look and to his credit, he did. Riley got out and gave us a casual wave before going around to pull out two suitcases from the

trunk. He'd sure as hell packed light. I felt like we might not be able to move around inside due to the extensive 'cover all bases' approach I'd taken to packing.
"Riley, hey," Freddie said, striding towards him with his hand extended. "I'm Freddie."
Riley shook his hand and smiled warmly.
"Good to meet you. Hey Steph. It's been a while."
"Yes it has," she smiled, as they came closer and shared a hug, "How's it going?"
"Good," he replied, finally looking at me and smiling. I smiled back and walked tentatively towards him.
"Hey," he nodded at me.
"Hi," I replied.
We got Riley's stuff loaded up and it was time to set off. We sat in the cab, gave Evan a wave goodbye and suddenly, I realised, this was it. We were off.
Beginning the road trip in our home town may not sound very exciting or worthwhile, but it is New York City after all! Like proper tourists, armed with a guidebook and map, we set off for the Statue of Liberty. We'd been told to do that first as it was one of the most popular places. I kept sneaking little glances at Riley. He really is beautiful. He has this face which is hard to find flaws in. I know that sounds silly, but believe me, it's true. And he was wearing a pair of (what looked like) vintage jeans, all frayed and faded, and a navy blue t-shirt with the Route 66 sign on the front. Simple, but ridiculously attractive. Steph called me on it a few times (the staring), but it was hard not to.
The thing that bothered me the most though was

that he'd hardly said two words to me. Sure, he'd said 'hey' when he arrived, but that hardly counts as a conversation, does it? And considering he knew me the best of all, he'd spent most of the time glued to Freddie's side, chatting and laughing with him. I wondered if maybe it wasn't such a good idea to invite him, then I looked at my watch and realised we were twenty-five minutes into a week-long road trip. That made me feel silly...and a little worried.
So after parking the motorhome, we caught the ferry to Liberty Island. It was busy, but it was also just after 11am and we were going to see the Statue of Liberty, so what did we expect? We were recognised in minutes, and spent most of the half an hour ride signing autographs and posing for photographs - we could hardly escape, could we?!
When we arrived, we kept our heads down and got in the queue for the elevator to the crown - there was no way I was going to climb 354 steps to the top! Freddie noticed the queue clock – two and a half hours.
"I have an idea," Riley said, going to take my hand. Suddenly he changed his mind and waved me on, which made me feel like I had the plague or something. I grudgingly followed him to the front of the queue, where a couple of people pointed and gossiped about us.
"Hey," Riley charmed to the lady at the door. As if on cue, a little girl hollered, "It's Riley Kitson! And Rebecca Russo!". With a quick glance, the lady recognised us and Riley smiled.
"What do you say? Just this once..."
The lady, obviously smitten by Riley's charm and

recognising at least one of us, relented.
"Normally I wouldn't let anyone do this but..."
We all smiled, thanked her and slipped inside.
Freddie high-fived Riley.
"Good plan," he congratulated, and Riley beamed before shrinking into his shell a bit and shrugging.
"No big deal," he said, then he smiled at Steph and followed her into the elevator as Freddie paid for us all. I might as well have not been there. What was his deal?
Still, I took a deep breath and focussed on where we were…the Statue of Liberty! Wow! We spent at least half an hour there, as the views were incredible. The skyline is totally different from there, like a picture postcard. It was hot and sunny too, so the sky was almost clear blue. We watched the Staten Island ferry go by, and generally gawped at New York City from afar. We took lots of pictures, then took one last look before heading back down.
We quickly realised that we all had different opinions as to where to go next, namely the boys wanting to go to Yankee Stadium and us girls wanting to do some more sight-seeing. Consulting the map as we perched it on a litter bin, we planned two routes. The boys would go to Yankee Stadium, whilst Steph and I would take a slow walk to Rockefeller Centre, taking in all the sights before we met there at 6:30pm. Steph and Freddie had a passionate kiss goodbye, leaving Riley and I to stare awkwardly at the traffic. We waved goodbye and consulted the guidebook.
Steph and I wandered around the city for a while and before we knew it, it was four o' clock. We still

had so much to do, so we hopped on the subway and hot-footed it to the Empire State Building. Deciding that we'd already been all the way to the top of somewhere high today, we took a couple of pictures from outside then took another subway to Grand Central (I'm still in awe of that place) and had a look at the Chrysler Building. Again, it seemed pointless to go up, especially as there isn't an observation deck, but we did go into the lobby to check out the mural on the ceiling, dedicated to 'transport and human endeavour' (so says the guidebook), which was pretty amazing. By now, we were understandably ravenous so we had some hot dogs before walking to St Patrick's Cathedral and onto Rockefeller Center. We reached it at 6:45pm.

The guys were waiting, both with Yankee caps and other souvenirs. At least we looked less touristy next to them! I asked Riley about it, just to make conversation, but it was more like small-talk and after a couple of minutes, we were left trailing awkwardly behind Freddie and Steph, who next to us looked like an over the top Las Vegas wedding couple. And to top it all off, I thought Rockefeller sucked. It was just a bunch of big buildings. Okay, the plaza was cool with the gold statue, but that was about it.

I wasn't in the highest of spirits but Freddie and Steph managed to get us to Times Square before dark and into a little place called The Jive Joint. I cheered up the second I walked through the door. A 1940's swing-dance club with a live orchestra. Like, hello? I was in heaven. To begin with, I felt a bit conscious of our sweaty day wear but it didn't

matter - everyone in the place was so cool. We had a beautiful meal and spent the next two hours hanging out, occasionally dancing and laughing. Riley finally began to loosen up around me, but I could still sense that something wasn't quite right. At about quarter to midnight, we all got a taxi back to the motorhome. We waved goodbye to NYC and set off for Trenton along Highway 1, with our first musical accompaniment being 'On A Day Like Today' by Bryan Adams. Most of the songs are about driving, or 'free is all you gotta be, dream dreams no one else can see', which I never paid attention to until that moment. Hmm.
It was a pretty uneventful journey, which I spent obsessing over whether or not to ask Riley if I could rest my head on his shoulder, or if I should just do it. I ended up doing neither and singing along to the music in my head. In fact, I don't think I even dared to look at him in case he saw me.
We stopped in Trenton, parked up in a quiet car-park next to a barber's shop and got ready for bed. A bed I was supposed to be sharing with Riley. I shiftily (and carefully) got changed, as did he, and we climbed into bed. A little fidgeting and adjusting the covers, as far apart in a small double bed as two people can be. I cannot do this for a whole week. No way.

JULY 20th

A lot can happen in an airless room in a motorhome after dark. No, we didn't *do* anything... But we did end up talking about what was going on.
You can't sleep side by side with someone and not touch them, or knock them as you roll over. After the third time of doing this and apologising, Riley spoke up.
"Don't apologise."
What can you say to that? I went the dumb route.
"Why not?"
"Because it's nothing to be apologetic about."
"Okay".
Silence. Eventually he sighed.
"Have I been acting weird today?"
I sighed, smiling.
"Yes!"
He smiled (so attractive, I can't tell you...).

"I'm sorry."
"Was it something I did?"
"Not really…"
I think I actually pressed a rewind button in my head, as images of the past day played in my mind. What had I done?
"So...what is it then?" I finally asked aloud. He looked around the room, then back at me.
"I guess I don't know how to be around you. Not after all that's happened between us."
I nodded to myself.
"Well, I guess we just need to draw a line under all that stuff," I suggested brightly. "What's in the past, you know, it's done. We're moving on."
"We are?" he asked, flashing me a hint of a smirk, which how I resisted kissing him is an unexplained mystery. I did, however, smile.
"Well, if not, then why did you want to come along?"
Riley's face grew serious. He stared up the ceiling as I stared at his brooding face.
"I always wanted to go on a road trip," he stated.
Huh. Not exactly the response I'd been hoping for.
"Me too," I agreed.
He turned his face towards me, his eyes grazing my face inquisitively.
"What?"
"Nothing," he replied, looking away again.
"So..." I said, trying to fill the awkward middle-of-the-night silence, "I mean, *we're* okay though, right?"
He smiled and nodded, an image that stayed in my head until I fell asleep, then he rolled over so his back was to me.

"Good night," he mumbled.
"Night."
I stared at the curve of his back for a while until the temptation to touch almost got the better of me, and I rolled over to face the other way. My heart was pounding but I didn't really know why. I eventually fell asleep.

***

When I woke up, I felt ready to get on with the trip. I had more energy and I felt a hell of a lot better about the whole Riley thing. We had a quick breakfast of cornflakes and coffee then set off for Philadelphia. I was about to put 'home', but strangely enough, I'm not sure whether it is now. Whatever. It's my home town, where my family and many of my friends still live. And that was why Steph, Freddie and I felt it only right to pay the city a visit.
First stop was Independence Hall. We had a look around, read the plaques on the walls about which room served what purpose, what crack was caused by what, who sneezed where (Freddie and I joked about that a lot, we had to keep stifling our giggles from the poor tour guide), then took a couple of pictures before going to look at the Liberty Bell. We then went to City Hall, and Philadelphia was done. We didn't see the point in hanging around any longer because we'd all grown up there, got the spangly t-shirt, etc. So we got back in the motorhome and put Lenny Kravitz on, setting off down the 95 Highway towards Baltimore.
As we entered Baltimore two hours later, it was

early evening, so we decided to have dinner and explore the town tomorrow.
It felt like a date. I don't know why, but my head was in the mentality of getting dolled up and going out to dinner like it was a date. But keeping that surprise of 'Wow, you look nice' is impossible in a 30-foot motorhome, believe me. So as Steph and I got dressed and did our make-up in my room, Riley kept flitting in and out. But he did keep giving me little glances (I saw him in the mirror as I did my mascara) and that gave me butterflies. It also made me feel great about how I looked - a dramatic change from a white vest and khaki cut-offs to a fuschia pink strappy dress with a frilled hem. Steph whispered to me, as the guys were down the other end,
"You do know how obvious it is that you want to jump each other?!"
I answered her with a shrug and a spritz of perfume.
“I'm not going to be the one to make the first move,” I told her. “If he wants me, he can sure as hell come and get me.”
Steph glanced down towards the boys.
“I guess it is only a 30 foot walk...”
I arched my eyebrow at her and she laughed.
“I wouldn't be worried about him not making a move,” she said with a smile. “I would be more worried about what you're going to do when he *does*.”
Our dinner was pretty eventful, but only in a small, incidental kind of way. Like, I still couldn't stop checking Riley out, especially since he was now all dressed up and his hair is just so ruffle-able (I don't

care if that's not a word, it's perfect). We kept knocking legs and feet under the table and we both ordered the same thing.... Do you see what I mean? Hardly any of this matters at all. I so need some kind of psychiatric help.
Anyway, we did have a very interesting conversation about who we'd dated, no holds barred, as far back as we could remember. Even though I thought I knew Freddie really well, it came to light that he'd cheated on his girlfriend a few years back with Melanie, my brother's fiance. Woah. It was a big revelation, but it wasn't so bad as Mel wasn't with David at the time. But the biggest thing to come from that conversation was hearing Riley's list. A few randoms before high school, Summer Delaney, the model...and that's it. Summer had been his girlfriend for 3 years. That's not even...I couldn't believe it. I mean, why would he break up with her? It must have been huge.
"No, not really. We just grew apart as the years went on. I mean, I still love her it's just we just didn't want to be together anymore."
Riley still loves Summer. Hmm.
That conversation totally freaked me out, and I felt like I was in direct competition. I mean, he'd only really dated her and me. I was praying there'd be no mentionitis - you know, 'Summer liked that', 'Summer would never wear that'. Dread set into the pit of my stomach.
After the meal, we went window-shopping for a while. We walked past this antiques shop, which had a brass statue in the window of two naked people, a man and woman, with their arms wrapped around each other as she gazed up into

his eyes. Riley stood next to me and grinned.
"Oh look honey, it's us."
I smirked.
"Yeah, that's about right. His hand is resting on her ass as she dreams of a day when he won't be so forthcoming."
It was Riley's turn to smirk.
"Nah, that isn't us…" (my heart sank) "Their asses are far less perky than ours."
We both laughed and he wrapped his arm around me, pulling me into him. It felt so good to have him hug me again. Not that I've replayed it in my head ninety times since it happened. Much.
Anyway, we continued to stroll along, me buying a pair of fading pink sunglasses ("So you can always see the world through rose-tinted glasses", Freddie joked) and Steph and I both bought some beaded friendship bracelets from a street seller before heading back.
When we went to bed, Riley and I lay there talking about all the places we wanted to visit during the trip. We'd certainly made some progress from last night's awkward bedtime routine. But I still couldn't stop thinking about Summer....

JULY 21st

We got up quite early, got dressed (it was really hot, so I chose a white sundress with embroidered blue flowers across the top) and had some breakfast before setting off into Baltimore.
We walked through Fell's Point, which is so busy (it's a port) but really laid-back at the same time. It has cobble-stone narrow streets, loads of bars and red-brick buildings. We got an ice-cream from a stall which quickly melted and covered us in sticky drips. Not a good start to the day. We got a bus to Mount Vernon Square, where we were taken aback by the Washington Monument, which is far bigger than we'd imagined it to be. We went to take a picture but realised we'd forgotten the camera. Oh well. Mount Vernon is lovely, so fashionable with lots of fancy architecture and at one end, a huge marble fountain and a bronze statue kind of like the one at Rockefeller Center. It was like we'd stepped back in time, especially when a horse

drawn carriage rolled by.
By now we were hungry so we stopped at a little café and had baguettes and salad, things like that. However, I noticed Steph and Freddie weren't their usual selves. I decided (smartly) not to say anything.
We went onto Oriole Park at Camden Yards. It's a baseball stadium, home of the Baltimore Orioles, and we decided to take the tour, which was excellent. The best part was the Eutaw Street promenade, which had brass plaques embedded into the sidewalk where the home-runs had cleared the fence. Really very cool.
Riley kept placing his hands either on my shoulders or at the base of my back, to steer me from place to place. I wished he didn't. It made me go all Jello-like and I couldn't concentrate… Okay, so I loved it. But he does make me feel like a giddy ten year old.
After the tour, my feet were absolutely throbbing and the straps from the wedges I'd stupidly chosen to wear (to match my outfit, not the agenda of the day) were giving me blisters. I was practically hobbling. And guess what happened next? Riley told me take off my sandals and carry them because he was going to piggyback me. It was just the sweetest thing. He carried me to the bus stop, then from the other bus stop back to the motorhome. Steph kept trying not to smile when she looked at us but I caught her looking a few times. Even Freddie looked bemused. But I didn't care. As we trudged along, I couldn't help my racing heart. I mean, his hands were on my thighs, my *bare* thighs, and I couldn't stop that gorgeous

aftershave smell invading my nostrils. Don't even get me started on our bodies being pressed together. I just prayed he couldn't feel my heart beating. Or at least, that his was doing the same. Oh, and when I wasn't thinking about him, I was worrying about my dress riding up…

When we got back, we piled into the front seat ready to set off again. I turned to Riley as I rubbed and inspected my feet.

"My little blistered feet are forever grateful," I said to him, as Steph discussed what CD to put on with Freddie. Riley let his hand rest briefly over my feet, that were tucked up and resting on the seat.

"You're welcome, little feet."

I smiled at him and he smiled back before winding down the window. In the space of three days, we'd gone from not speaking to grand romantic gestures (at least, I thought so). Not bad…

It only took us about 40 minutes to get from Baltimore to Washington, but like last night, we arrived too late to do anything except grab dinner. We had the best night so far…then it all went horribly wrong. But first I'll detail all the good bits. We ate at this beautifully luxurious restaurant called The Monument. It had this huge elegant dining room with a marble fireplace and big traditional American paintings: it looked like a room in the White House or something. The food was absolutely delicious. I had fillet of steak with an entrecôte sauce, with chipped roast potatoes on the side. It was divine. Freddie ordered a rack of lamb, but I swear it was more like a rack of giant sheep! It was enormous! We all just giggled when they brought it out. But the funniest thing was that

he practically finished it all anyway.
During the meal, Riley kept up a proper British upper-crust accent, even when the waiter came out. I was in stifled hysterics, which got even more uncontrollable when I caught Steph's eye. He was hilarious. To finish off the meal, we had hazelnut chocolate bars with an espresso sauce, which was totally eye-opening and gave us that extra hit of energy we needed for our planned bar-hop that night.
We had four places we wanted to go to. The first was called Hometown, a relatively large bar with brick walls and little old-fashioned black and white photographs on the walls. But the best part about it was there were more than 200 brands of beers on sale. Freddie couldn't contain his excitement as he flashed his new ID (thank you for a conveniently timed June birth, Mrs King). Riley tried some French lager and extended the glass to me.
"You have to try some, Beccy," he enticed, in such a sexy, heart-melting way I could almost see him perfecting it in front of the mirror.
"You know it's illegal," I joked. "I couldn't possibly. It would be against my strict Christian upbringing."
Riley smiled and held it closer to me.
"Just drink it."
So I did. I had the biggest gulp I could manage, then wiped my mouth and looked up at him like a toddler trying to impress their Daddy. Riley patted my head, reading my mind and playing along.
"Good girl," he smiled, as he drank some and looked around the bar.
The next place we went to was the Rumba Lounge, totally hip with a Latin jazz vibe. Freddie went to

get us cocktails as we bagged a nice big leather sofa in the corner. Riley sat down, arm over the back, looking to the left. I hovered as Steph sat down at the other end, then thankfully he looked up at me.
"Well, come sit down then," he smiled, and so I did.
Steph budged into me as Freddie came back and gave us a cocktail each. I got the Citrus Spangler (totally gorgeous) and a chance to sit as close to Riley without us actually merging into one another.
I casually chatted to Steph for a while, as he and Freddie leaned forward and chatted over us.
After a while, we sat back together, with Freddie and Steph chatting (and kissing) and Riley and I chatting (and *not* kissing, regretfully). Somehow we ended up talking about ex's again.
"I just can't believe that Summer was your only girlfriend," I admitted.
"Until you," Riley noted, making my heart pound.
"Okay, so…why me?" I said, just putting it out there.
"Why you? What do you mean, 'why you?'," he asked back.
I took a sip of my Citrus Spangler and ran my fingers through my hair.
"Well, it just seems to me that going from having a steady, beautiful" (I had to say it, just to see) "girlfriend to not having one would be a big deal."
Riley looked at me. That made me feel very uneasy.
He was just *looking* at me…
"Yeah, I guess it was," he finally said. "So…how does this relate to us going out?"
I suddenly felt really stupid, a clichéd crazy-girl.
But I just couldn't just leave it there. I had to make it seem that I wasn't completely out of my mind.

"I just meant that, well, going from Summer to me...we seem totally different. I mean, she's..."
I faded out, wishing I could turn back time and just scrap this entire conversation. Riley gently flicked my hair.
"Blonde, and you're brunette," he noted.
I smiled.
"Yeah but...okay, forget I ever said anything," I mumbled, caving into my unfounded insecurities.
Riley nodded and finished off his sangria. I sunk lower into the chair and looked the other way.
What a fool.
Luckily Steph decided we should go onto the next bar so we got a taxi to Gravity (being cramped next to Riley felt claustrophobic this time) and wow, was it worth the effort. As we walked in, Steph linked arms with me.
"Wow! This place is like, retro heaven!"
She wasn't wrong. It was very minimalistic, all white, black and chrome, with mod Sixtie's bar stools.
"Look!" Riley exclaimed, pointing to a projection of kung-fu movies on the far wall. The place was pretty crowded and everyone there was young, beautiful and looking at us. Steph leaned closer and whispered,
"Giggle. Now."
I obeyed, and we looked like we didn't have a care in the world. It always works, and slowly people turned back to their conversations and forgot about us. We made our way straight to the bar (it was packed though, so it was more like a crooked line) and ordered a cocktail in a fishbowl. I'd never seen anything like it! It sure was heavy. We made our

way to a slightly less crowded area and stood in a circle.
"Oh, definitely," I said, reading everyone's faces. Freddie started, as we chanted him on. Steph went next, spluttering as it ran down her face and passed it to me. I quickly glanced around the circle before downing the equivalent of like, an entire ordinary glass worth of beer, before handing it to Riley as I wiped my mouth. It was all over the top of my white dress but I didn't care. We cheered as Riley finished the glass and laughed, wrapping his arm around me and stumbling as I steadied to keep us upright in a haze of drunken giggles.
As if we needed to go onto another bar. I think if we'd have ended the night there, the bad stuff would never have surfaced…
Still. We did.
It was called Amigos. By now, we were definitely 'merry' on our way to 'blind drunk'. Steph even tripped as she climbed out of the taxi, which sent me and Freddie into side-splitting laughter as Riley helped her up, he too giggling. Steph was the only one not laughing.
The dance floor was small and totally packed, but we weaved our way in anyway, dancing to salsa remixes of J-Lo and Ricky Martin. Riley and I were outrageously flirting as we bumped and grinded. All of a sudden, Freddie grabbed my arm and pulled me from Riley.
"We're leaving," he shouted above the music. Riley quickly followed as I wriggled free from Freddie's rip, automatically thinking he was being over-protective. I clung to Riley's arm.
"No way, we're fine," I declared, as Freddie looked

at Riley.
"Dude, we need to go. Now."
Riley steered me out as I drunkenly protested and dragged my heels. Eventually, he wrapped his arms around my waist and hoisted me into the air over his shoulder, carrying me out of the club.
"Put me DOWN!" I demanded angrily as we went from the sticky heat inside to the cool air outside. It was then that I noticed Steph vomiting over the kerb.
"Oh my God!" I said, stumbling down next to her and pulling her hair back off her face. "Are you okay?"
"I hate him," she told me.
"Who?"
"Freddie," she hissed. I looked over my shoulder where Freddie had his arms folded and was looking nervously at us.
"What did you do?" I demanded, as Freddie exploded.
"Nothing!"
Riley called a cab as I helped Steph to her feet.
"Yes you did! She was all over you and you were, like...well, you were all over her too!"
"I was not! *She* came onto *me*. I was trying to get away from her but it was too crowded and...."
"You're a liar!" Steph hollered, as people began to stop and see what the fuss was about. I looked to Riley for support. He opened the door to the taxi and calmly steered Freddie into it. I pushed Steph's hair out of her face as I told her,
"Let's just get back to the motorhome and we can sort it out there, okay?"
She looked very pale so I quickly got into the taxi

next to Riley, as Steph took the front seat and sat with her arms folded. The atmosphere was icy to say the least.
When we got back, all hell broke loose. They screamed at each other, Freddie protesting his innocence as Steph started crying but still shouting hysterically. Steph had totally overreacted to Freddie and some girl who'd been dancing with him and kissed him on the cheek. But the real reason she was so mad came to the surface with the revelation she'd been totally bugged about him and Melanie...and the fact that she hadn't known about it. Freddie came back at her about Seth, and it just got totally out of control with Steph telling him she couldn't be with someone she didn't trust and him telling her he wouldn't stay with her if she still had feelings for Seth.
Thankfully, they both believed in not going to bed until it was sorted out…which is where Riley and I came in. We calmed them down and explained it all to them, from the blown-out-of-proportion incident at Amigos to ex-relationships being over and in the past. Finally, after far too many unnecessarily hurtful words, they made up with a long, tender kiss. Then they gave us both hugs and went off for a walk.
Riley and I collapsed in our room and began giggling. It sure had been a crazy night. Then I rolled onto my side, ran my fingers through his hair and kissed him. I just *kissed* him.
To my blurry-eyed surprise, he pushed me away said,
"No, you're drunk."
I kissed him again, and he rolled me onto my back.

"No. We can't. Not like this."
"Oh, come on, Riley. Kiss me."
Riley sighed and stroked my hair off my face.
"You're drunk and we're not doing this."
With that, he got up and left, leaving me all alone in the motorhome. I felt sad, then stupid, then angry…then very drunk and tired. I fell asleep quickly after that.

JULY 22nd

I had the worst headache this morning, and teamed with being absolutely ravenous but having a horrible feeling of regret settled deep inside the pit of my stomach, I just wanted to stay in bed all day. Alone.

But I couldn't. I had to get up and face the music. Riley was wearing a baseball cap and a hoody, sitting hunched over a bowl of Cheerio's. I too had dressed how I felt, wearing dungarees over a vest, all my hair and face hidden under a floppy khaki hat. I grabbed a Pop Tart and waited in silence until it popped from the toaster, then I took it and ate it in the front cab of the motorhome.

I had just finished when Riley opened the door beside me. He rested his arms on the seat, his chin on top. As he looked up at me, even the hangover from hell couldn't detract my attention from his puppy-dog eyes and pout.

"I just wanted to apologise. I acted like a jerk last night."
I squinted in the sun and looked down at him.
"I think that's my line."
He smiled and held out his hand.
"Friends?"
"Friends," I said, shaking it. But I still felt totally weirded out being in his presence.
This weird feeling lasted all day. We went to The Mall, looked at the Capitol Building and took a walk around the Lincoln Memorial, before making our way to the White House. That was really interesting. We went to the East Room, the Green Room (the walls are made of green silk!), the Blue Room and we went up to the Oval Office, but we're not allowed into the West Wing. Still, it was amazing. You felt totally privileged to be there.
Of course, I also spent a lot of time watching Riley. I felt so dumb for kissing him. Just when everything was starting to go right too… I bet Summer would never have done anything as stupid as that. And to top it all off, Freddie and Steph were so sickeningly together I felt like a social outcast. I eventually told her what had happened and she was totally supportive, sticking by me for the rest of the day.
We left Washington just after four o' clock. We were all still pretty full from lunch, so that meant a six hour drive to Charleston.
It was our first real taster at solid driving and the road trip was really kind of christened during this drive. Our first four cities had been relatively close together, but now we were beginning to venture further afield. I still had a headache, so I wasn't

really up for talking. I put my new sunglasses on, sat back and just rested. The motion of the motorhome constantly moving was bad for my head, but relaxing in another way because I could concentrate on that instead of the fact that Riley was sat pressed up against my side.

We pulled into a service station about halfway and got a couple of bags of chips and a pack of six Cokes. Freddie filled up the tank as Steph got the food, leaving Riley and I alone for a couple of minutes. I had no idea what to say, and I sensed he was afraid to speak first too.

"This is stupid," I said quietly. "We can't go through this road trip barely speaking to each other."

"Yeah, you're right," Riley agreed.

But that was it. We still didn't talk. It was so very awkward.

We set off again, the atmosphere in the cab very, very quiet. The gentle motion of the drive sent me to sleep and when I woke up, we were just pulling to a stop in Charleston. I looked up at Riley, who I was slumped against, and he smiled down at me and yawned. I guess he'd nodded off too. I looked over at Freddie and smiled as I stretched and yawned too.

"You must be exhausted," I said.

He rubbed his eyes with one hand and nodded, pulling the keys out of the ignition.

"In a word, yes."

Riley opened the door and we climbed out. I checked my watch as we stretched and yawned some more. It was quarter to eleven.

"I'm going straight to bed," Steph announced, tugging on Freddie's hand, who waved at us. She

opened the door to the living quarters and they disappeared inside.
"Night you guys," Freddie called behind him, and we chorused back,
"Night."
Riley and I looked at each other then he gestured at the door. I nodded and went first, as he followed me down towards our bedroom. We got changed and crawled into bed, then Riley yawned out loud.
"I am totally wasted."
"Me too," I agreed.
I turned onto my side, my back to him and closed my eyes. I listened as he shifted about then realised he was hovering over me. I rolled onto my back and looked up, his face just inches from mine. I wondered if he was going to kiss me when he began to speak.
"Do you think we could just forget this day, and last night, ever happened?"
I rolled my eyes and put my hands up to cover my face, nodding my head behind it.
"Yes, *please,*" I mumbled.
Riley's hands pulled mine down between us and we stared at each other. Then he cleared his throat, rolling back to lay on his back. I turned and rolled over to face the other way again.
"Good night, Riley."
I think I heard him sigh before he replied,
"Good night, Beccy."
So far, the road trip hadn't gone exactly to plan. But I was still hopeful that things would start to get better between us and as I closed my eyes, and remembered what day it was tomorrow, I wished myself an early birthday wish.

JULY 23rd

I desperately wanted a lie-in today. What I did get, though, was Riley gently rousing me from my sleep by stroking my cheek. As I squinted in the morning sunlight, he smiled.
"Happy birthday, butterfly."
I smiled before realising how awful I must have looked. It was first thing in the morning, after all. I pulled the sheet up over my head and murmured something about leaving me to sleep. He got up and playfully patted my thighs on the way out.
"C'mon Beccy," he said cheerfully. "It's your birthday, it's a beautiful, sunny day, and we've got the whole of Charleston to explore."
I got up and dressed and after my birthday hugs from Steph and Freddie, I was practically hustled out of the door without so much as a glass of OJ. Where was my birthday breakfast?
We spent the morning up until lunch touring the

town centre. Charleston is very historic-looking, with lots of lovely views and churches and museums all over the place. As we strolled around, it felt more like we were in a little French market-town than three days from New York City. Like in Baltimore, we got ice-creams from a street vendor and strolled along the harbour. We laughed and talked like old friends (which I guess we are) and stopped to look at the Fort Sumter National Monument, where the first shot of the Civil War was fired. Riley was on top form, making us all laugh. Freddie and Steph were cute but not sickly sweet, and for once, I was totally at ease with everyone and everything.
For lunch we had pasta and pizza at a little Italian café, then we got a taxi to Middleton Place, the country's oldest landscaped gardens. We didn't really go there to appreciate the hundreds of types of flowers; we went there to have a laid back stroll in the sunshine. And that's what we got. We took it in turns to walk around with each other. I started with Steph and we had a good girly chat about everyone we saw, what they were wearing, stuff like that. And of course, we talked about Riley.
"You two looked so cute together, your heads resting against each other," Steph cooed about last night. I smiled and shrugged.
"Well, embarrassingly he now knows I like him..."
"How's that?" Steph asked, and I reminded her of our drunken almost-kiss.
"Well, do you know how *he* feels?"
"Not exactly. We seem to take one step forwards and then other one straight back. It's exhausting."
Steph sighed and put her arm supportively around

me.
"Don't worry about it, babe. You'll find out one way or another."
Then she leaned in close and lowered her voice.
"But I'm almost certain he's into you in a big way."
I walked along with Freddie next. As we bumbled along, commenting on the grounds and the flowers, he said,
"So c'mon. Tell me all about you and Riley. I know you're dying too."
I laughed.
"What's there to say? You've been there for most of it."
"Ooh," he grinned, "*most* of it, huh? What don't I know about?"
I laughed and gave him a playful shove, to which he retaliated by putting his arm around my shoulder. I wrapped my arm loosely around his waist and we continued to walk.
"I haven't got a clue how he really feels about me. I mean, okay, yeah, so we flirt. But that can be a totally empty gesture. Something's holding him back...I just don't know what."
"How do you feel about him?"
"I'm totally into him. I don't think I love him, not yet anyway. Not like how I loved Josh. But I've got the *biggest* crush on him. I just can't take my eyes off him..."
We broke into song, singing 'You're Just Too Good To Be True', until we faded out and Freddie said,
"Well, let's just say I'd be blind, and very stupid, not to notice that you two have a lot of chemistry. And trust me, he gets all the messages you're sending his way."

My heart fluttered a bit as I looked up at Freddie. "That's all very well, but how does he feel about me?"
Freddie shrugged.
"Sorry, sweetie, he hasn't said anything to me. I guess he knows I'd come running to tell you."
I sighed and scuffed my feet along the path. If only I knew for sure how he felt...
By the time Riley and I were alone together, it was late in the afternoon, my feet were beginning to ache and I was more confused than ever. I tried not to blush when he walked my way in a vest and khaki shorts, his lovely ruffle-able hair tucked under his baseball cap, and I tried even harder to prevent my heart from going into a coronary seizure.
"Well, hello sweetie," he said in that fake British accent again. "It's just so fabulous to see you."
He took my arms in his hands and kissed the air either side of my face. I stifled a giggle as I replied, "Oh, and I should say the same for you, darling. You're looking bronzed and healthy. Have we been to the spa again?"
Riley linked arms with me and walked us along like a couple of old ladies.
"Well, of course, dear. One has to make an effort with one's appearance."
"One must," I agreed, and looked up at him. He squinted in the sun and looked down, biting his lip and making him look about a hundred times sexier than he already did. We both laughed.
"Classic," I sighed, as he dropped my arm and pushed his hands into his pockets, kicking a stone ahead of us. All of a sudden, a peacock stepped out

in front of us from behind a hedge and let out an almighty screech. We both jumped back and half-shrieked, before sighing and laughing as it ruffled its feathers and trotted off in the opposite direction. I clung to Riley's arm as we laughed and walked ahead again.
"So what did you talk about with the others?"
I casually dropped his arm and readjusted the halterneck tie of my top, my heart pounding nervously inside my ribcage.
"Oh, this and that," I lied smoothly. "What about you?"
He smirked down at me.
"This and that."
Two small children ran down the path towards us laughing, the smallest toddling along in a pretty pink sundress and matching hat.
"Oh, sweet," I said, as they ran right between us.
"Yeah, she's gorgeous," Riley agreed. Then he looked at me and tugged on the peak of his cap.
"We would have really beautiful children," he said, totally taking me by surprise. I raised an eyebrow and looked up at him.
"You think?"
"Oh, totally."
We continued to walk and I said,
"So you would want to, I mean…you think we could? Like, make good parents?"
Riley slowed to a stop and took me by the arms. As he leaned down to look at me straight in the eyes, I was paralysed with fear and anticipation about what he might say.
"Beccy? You would make the best mother in the world. It would be an honour to have children with

you."
It was intense for all of about, three seconds, then he let me go and continued to walk. I skipped to fall into step with him again and we walked in silence before he said, grinning down at me,
"I mean, you'd be a natural. Look at your great child-bearing hips."
He broke into a laugh and I gasped, laying a series of slaps into him, chasing him up the path. He turned and grabbed me by the waist, laughing,
"Ooh, let me touch those child-bearing hips! I love your child-bearing hips!"
I eventually gave him a hard shove then stood, hands on hips, in a mock-serious angry pose.
"That's *so* not funny, Riley."
He pouted, dropped his shoulders and opened his arms.
"I'm sorry, butterfly. You know I'm just teasing you."
I let a smile spread across my face before stepping into a full embrace and savouring every second of it. Then he grabbed my hips, making me jump, and shrieked,
"Oh, your lovely child-bearing hips are glorious to hold!"
I mean, *c'mon...*

***

We got back to the motorhome at half past five and got changed into our evening wear before parking the motorhome in the car-park of Wildwood Mansion, where we'd booked a room for the evening. We checked in and argued over the rooms

(I wanted to share with Steph but she was desperate for some 'quality time' with Freddie) then got settled in. It had been stupid of us to get ready for dinner so early because once in the room, and upon finding it had its own whirlpool in the bathroom, we had to get undressed and into our swimwear to take full advantage of the situation. So there we were, Riley and I, in a hotel whirlpool. *Alone*. The sexual tension was electric.
"Okay," Riley confessed, over the sound of the radio playing in the background, "I so badly want to jump you right now."
I grinned and nodded.
"The feeling is mutual, Mr Kitson."
“So what are the chances of me seeing the birthday girl in her birthday suit?”
I locked my eyes on him and smirked, before giving him a wink and sliding down into the water, soaking my hair through before coming back up and sleeking it down.
"God, this feels so good after being stuck in that cramped, sweaty motorhome."
Riley nodded and stretched his arms out along the side of the bath.
"You can say that again."
We sat for a while, listening to the music, then we just looked at each other. We smiled, then I sighed.
"I can't for the life of me figure you out."
He looked confused.
"Figure *me* out…? I'd have thought my earlier statement made things pretty clear.”
"No, like how you *really* feel about me. What you want out of all this. You're one of very few people I can't figure out just by looking at them."

He smirked.
"Yeah, well... you'll just have to keep trying then, won't you?"
I smirked back and replied,
"Or I could just give up altogether."
Then I climbed gracefully out of the tub and walked, in my soaking wet bikini, across the bathroom and into the bedroom, grabbing a towel on the way. Smooth...
We got ready again for dinner and I blow-dried my hair which, if I do it just right, makes it go all wavy. It worked, and I emerged clean and elegant in my white sundress, with wavy hair resting on my shoulders. When you feel good about how you look, you feel good in every way. I felt as though I had Riley wrapped around my little finger for a change.
The night got off to a good start when Freddie and Steph both wide-eyed me as we walked towards them.
"Someone looks good tonight," Steph remarked. I love her. What are best friends for, except giving you compliments in front of your crush? Freddie looked over my head and around us, going,
"Who? Where?"
I gave him a playful shove and he grinned at me.
"Nah, you look great."
I curtseyed briefly and smiled.
"Thank you."
Then I looked at Riley (who also looked pretty fine) and said,
"One does have to make an effort with one's appearance."
As he slid his hand across my bare shoulders and

pulled me close to whisper, "One certainly has", I tried not to grin like a Cheshire Cat.
We had dinner at the hotel restaurant, which was pretty upmarket. We ate steak and duck instead of cheeseburgers, and drank wine instead of Coke. Still, it made for a pretty special birthday meal, and Freddie and Steph gave me their presents. I got nothing from Riley, which he apologised for, saying he hadn't even known it was my birthday until Steph told him last night. Typical guy. It was kind of disappointing, but he made up for it by playing footsie with me under the table the entire time. We were definitely both aware of it because every so often, one of us would move them slightly then put them straight back. *And* we kept exchanging flirty glances too. I was starting to believe in birthday wishes...
After dinner, which was probably about nine o' clock, we went for another stroll along the town harbour. A lot of bars were open, but only a few gift shops, so we looked in them. As I studied the jewellery in the window of a little rustic shop, I felt Riley's presence behind me and his hand on my waist.
"Let me buy you a birthday present," he said.
My heart was all over the place, and beating very fast. He was going to give me a heart attack if he wasn't careful.
"What would you like?" he continued. "How about a ring?"
As I scanned my eyes over the jewellery case, he walked towards the entrance declaring,
"It's okay. I've found something better."
Freddie and Steph wandered over and I smiled,

whispering,
"He's just gone to buy me something! He's going to buy me a ring!"
Their eyes grew wide as they looked at me, then each other, then continued walking as Riley bounded back out of the shop. He held his hand out innocently with a little gift-wrapped package on it.
"Happy birthday."
I grinned and took it, turning round to open it as we followed Steph and Freddie along the street. It was a little box. Maybe he had bought me a ring after all…
"Go on! Open it then," he urged.
It was a wooden box, the same size as a ring box but as I opened it, my heart racing, I found a wooden ladybug with wiggly legs that jiggled when you moved it. Inside the lid it said 'I Luv U'. It was the sweetest, silliest gift I'd ever received, and so much better than a ring. It was *so* Riley. I grinned up at him and stopped walking.
"Thank you," I said and he shrugged.
"It's not a butterfly, but it's close enough," he mumbled, and I smiled reassuringly.
"It's perfect. And you were right, it's *so* much better than a ring."
His face broke into a wide smile and he nodded once, definitely.
"I thought so too," he announced triumphantly, before wrapping his arm around my shoulders. I put my hand on his waist (how I love to hold onto his warm, taut waist) and we caught up with Freddie and Steph. We were walking along like two couples now. But I was just happy to 'be' with

Riley and not rush into labelling it. Not today. Besides, everyone knows the chase is far more fun than the kill - even if it is prime meat like Riley! We sat out on the harbour until we got tired, then we walked back to Wildwood Mansion and said goodnight, before crawling into bed. They were such *good* beds. And my love bug sat proudly on my bedside table, watching us as we slept.

JULY 24th

When I woke up, I felt Riley roll over to his side of the bed. I pulled the sheet up instinctively over me and yawned, rubbing my eyes. Had he been watching me sleep?
"Morning," I said, rolling over to face him. He sat up and I looked contentedly at the curve of his back.
"Yeah, morning," he mumbled. "Do you mind if I take the first shower?"
I shook my head and rolled back over to the face the balcony.
"No, of course not."
"Okay, cool," he muttered, as he went into the bathroom. I heard the shower turning on so I clicked on the radio alarm clock beside the bed and looked at the love bug. I smiled. Last night had been blissful. I went from station to station, until I found WATC playing 'Amazed' by Lonestar. As I

lay there listening to it on our comfy bed, the sun streaming in through the balcony doors, just listening to Riley in the shower…it was so peaceful. Until my stomach rumbled.

"Riley, do you want me to order some breakfast?" I called out, as the sound of water stopped.

"Like, room service? Sure. Do whatever you want."

So I ordered two rounds of toast and tea with croissants and fresh fruit. Just as there was a knock at the door, Riley emerged from the bathroom, towel round his waist, hair dropping wet. I could hardly breathe.

"That's been charged to your room, madam," the waiter told me.

"Uh, yeah, thanks," I mumbled, as he wheeled the trolley in and parked it by the bed.

"Yummy," Riley said, as I tipped the waiter and closed the door behind him.

"How was the shower? Is it a good one?"

Riley sat down and squinted one eye.

"Well, it's kind of…mad. But you can see for yourself. Come and have some breakfast first," he said, patting the bed beside him. How very, very tempting, I thought as I sat down to eat.

Riley wasn't wrong about the breakfast (it *was* yummy) nor was he wrong about the shower. Mad was a total understatement. The shower head was attached to a fixture that you could angle, but I couldn't sort it out so it was all over the place. Then I bashed my head on the perspex door as I reached for the shampoo and to top it all off, I didn't realise you had to take the metal plug thing out the plughole so the bottom filled up with so much water, I thought I was going to flood the bathroom.

I have never been so relieved to be patting my face dry with a towel, wrapped in another one, perched on the toilet with the lid down. I laughed to myself at the total joke of a shower I'd just had, then got dry and walked carefully into the bedroom. The bed had been made, the blankets folded neatly on the end. My clothes were piled on the chair by the dressing table, but everything belonging to Riley had gone. I felt abandoned, then kind of confused. I got dressed into my dungarees and flowery halter-neck as quickly as possible, half expecting him to walk in as I put on my underwear or something. But he didn't. I pulled a pink bandanna out of my bag and put it on over my still wavy hair. I packed up my stuff then took the love bug from the side and placed it safely in the front pocket of my dungarees before heading along the hall to Steph and Freddie's room. I knocked but there was no answer. So I went downstairs to the restaurant, trying to stay calm, where they were all sitting in the corner drinking coffee. I definitely sighed a little with relief.
"Look who decided to show," Freddie joked, as I made my way towards the table. I looked at Riley, who smiled.
"You didn't forget the love bug, did you?"
I smiled and patted the pocket it was in.
"It's as safe as can be," I replied, taking the seat beside him and smiling at Steph.
We piled back into the motorhome ready for our drive to Cincinnati. I decided I wanted to sit next to Freddie for a change (which I think took Riley by surprise a little bit) so Steph and I swapped places. As we set off, I nudged Freddie's leg with mine.

"You really are an angel for doing this, Freddie."
He grinned and checked the wing mirror.
"I know. Where would you be without me?"
Steph and I looked at each other before chorusing, "New York."
I smiled and put the radio on. I rested my feet up on the dash, tapping my toes inside my shoes and nodding my head to the beat as we set off along the highway.
We happily drove along, the towns, fields and signposts zipping past as quickly as they appeared. Because we'd been in each other's company 24/7 for six days, we didn't have much to talk about except to point something out or ask each other what music to listen to, so it was quiet ride along the 64 Interstate.
Not much happened with Riley either. Because we weren't sitting next to each other, and no one was talking, there was no flirty conversation or brushing of limbs. I did, however, catch his eye after leaning forwards to tie up my shoelace. We looked at each other, I smiled a little bit, so did he, then he rolled his eyes as his face broke into a smallish grin. I sat back and began twiddling with my hair. Our weird flirting-only relationship was equal parts fun and totally annoying….and that in itself was confusing, tiresome but totally addictive.
When we finally reached Cincinnati, it was about four o' clock. I got out of the cab and went round to the other side. As I stretched my arms above my head, Riley grabbed me by the waist, making me shriek. I held onto his hands with mine, my heart racing, as he wrapped his arms around my middle and snuggled into my neck. We half-waddled

towards the now open side door. It was a really tender, sweet moment, one that you wanted to last. But as we climbed the steps, he released me…only to slap my ass. I turned around and shot him a look, to which he innocently pouted, hands up, and grinned oh-so-sexily. I rolled my eyes and walked down to our bedroom, secretly loving it all.
Without warning, he grabbed me around the middle and carried me down to our bedroom, throwing me onto the bed like a ragdoll. I bounced and looked up at him with a gasp frozen across my face. I watched as Riley simply resumed his attack, clambering onto the bed on his knees and launching himself at me, pinning me to bed and tickling me. I giggled and eventually wriggled free of his grip, going straight for his very ticklish knees. He succumbed immediately to my counter-attack until finally, we stopped to catch our breath.
"How did you remember I have ticklish knees?" he asked me.
What do you say to that? I just shrugged.
"I guess it's kind of like battle tactics. Desperate times call for desperate measures."
Riley gave me that squinty, small smile look again and I called him on it.
"Stop giving me that look."
It caught him off-guard and I think I saw him blush.
"What look?"
"*That* look," I said, mimicking it then grinning.
"I didn't even realise I was doing it," he said, although I didn't quite believe him. As we waited silently, I began to hum 'Nothing Better Than A Double Bed', which he recognised, and we both

sung along to our favourite Cherry Soda song. We smiled at each other, then he sat forward and lunged at me, and I caught his hands with mine, our fingers slotting together. He had the strength and posture to beat me so he pushed me onto my back and pinned me to the bed. As he straddled me, he pretended to bite my nose a few times then we grinned at each other. It was a good job I didn't close my eyes or pout my lips for a kiss because instead, he rolled onto his back beside me. We lay side by side, just taking it all in, a little out of breath and very out of our depth. Then I reached into my pocket and pulled out the love bug. I opened it, holding it above us in the air. Riley reached over to prod it and its little legs jiggled.

"Have you named it?" he asked. I looked at him and creased my eyebrows.

"Have I *named* it?" I asked back.

"Yeah. Don't you girls do that? Like, name all your teddy bears and gifts and stuff."

I let out a laugh.

"Nooo..." I giggled.

He smiled and I wiggled the love bug.

"But if I did, I'd call it..." I began, as the door opened and Freddie and Steph came in. We wriggled to sit up as they came towards us, both wearing knowing smiles. Steph waved the guidebook then dropped it on the bed as she sat down.

"Sorry to interrupt, but there's a couple of parks we figured we could go to being as it's still light out," she told us. "Then we can go to the Newport Aquarium tomorrow."

I nodded once.

"Well, someone's got a plan."
Freddie smiled at Steph.
"That's my girl."
I climbed off the bed and headed for the door, grabbing Steph's hand and pulling her with me.
"We'll be getting ready next door so no distractions, okay? We need to make ourselves beautiful."
"How many hours do you think that will take?"
Freddie smirked at me and I rolled my eyes.
I fake-smiled and kicked out at him with my foot before going down the hall to the other bedroom. I rolled my eyes at Steph and we both grinned.

***

Twenty five minutes later, we were ready. Steph looked casually stunning, her hair in natural blonde waves wearing a black top and denim skirt. She'd chosen for me the shortest of mini's, a denim US flag print, with a red low-cut top. She'd also straightened my hair, waxed my legs and bronzed me up.
"And my work here is done," she declared, clapping her hands together. I glanced in the mirror and smiled.
"You look dynamite!" she added, and I grinned.
We emerged to find the guys ready and waiting.
Freddie low-whistled and I definitely saw Riley sit up straight.
"It's Rebecca Russo," Freddie said. "The hottest of the hot."
I giggled as Steph went over and wrapped her arms around him, clearing her throat and arching an eyebrow.

"Except for you, of course, my little molten lava lover."
I glanced at Riley, who raised both his eyebrows at me, and I giggled. We all set off, Riley quickly finding himself close enough to put his hands on my waist and steer me out of the motorhome.
Now every girl likes to be appreciated when they've put in the effort. I mean, if all it takes is a short skirt and a slick of lipstick to make the guy see the girl in a different light, then how can that be a bad thing, right? Well, I'm not so sure anymore. It felt great to be appreciated but it had such a falsity to it, very vain and testosterone-charged. What I mean is, Riley treated me like a queen, like his girlfriend-cum-prized possession, all night. Every excuse he could to touch me, or pull on my hand, or touch my back or shoulders, he took it without hesitation. We got a lot of glances and whispers, probably to do with who we were but also because we looked like the celebrities we were supposed to be, and not the travelling tourists we'd spent the rest of the trip as. Riley also acted a little… not jealous, but kind of possessive. Like a group of rowdy guys wolf-whistled after they'd passed us in the park. Steph and I found it amusing and harmless. Riley did not. He turned around, walking backwards and gave them a kind of threatening 'yeah, try it' look. I hit his back and he turned back around. I gave him a bemused smirk, to which he just draped his arm around my shoulders and shrugged it off with a 'Stupid little boys' comment. Hmm.
After our walk, we went for a meal in the Montgomery Inn. We all had barbecued food, as

everything on the menu it seemed was barbecued. But the best part of the night was sitting out on the deck at sunset, drinking fresh lemonade as the boats rolled by on the Ohio River. It was honestly as beautiful as it sounds. And with Riley outrageously flirting, and Steph and Freddie in high spirits, it was a perfect evening in so many ways.

Later in bed, as we lay side by side, I thought about everything that had happened between us in the last few days. From the gifts to the flirty banter, the piggyback rides to the mood swings. It was insane and unexplainable but being that we'd ended up exactly how we were then, lying side by side and (very probably) thinking about each other, I wouldn't have changed a thing. Except maybe that we would have been lying in each other's arms instead of lying side by side. Still, there was always tomorrow...

JULY 25th

I woke up hot, tired and achy. We got up, showered and got dressed (a bikini top under dungarees and *comfortable* sneakers, not wedges), deciding on having breakfast in a nearby café. To taste genuine pancakes oozing with maple syrup after such a long time (okay, like a week) was practically orgasmic. Then we headed to Newport Aquarium, taking in all the shops that had been closed last night. We were looking in this little hat and bag shop when Riley took a huge floppy sunhat and placed it on my head. He came round to look at me, tugging on the sides as I smiled sweetly at him. He grinned and nodded.
"That is the cutest thing ever. You *have* to buy it."
I pulled it off my head and looked at it. It was a dusky sandy pink, reversible with one side plain and one side Hawaiian print. It was quite nice... I

placed it back on the stand.
"No, I've got plenty of hats," I said, as Riley picked it up again and held it out for me to take.
"Either you buy it or I do," he stated, and I raised my eyebrows. I took it from him and put it on again, looking in the mirror. It did look quite nice…
Riley took it off me, reaching into the back pocket of his khaki shorts to produce his wallet. Walking towards the counter, I followed him as he handed the hat over to the shop assistant.
"Riley, you've already bought me enough," I argued.
"The love bug? Get real. This is just a present from me to you," Riley smiled, handing over a ten dollar bill to pay for it. The assistant smiled at me and I smiled back, then looked at Riley.
"Would you like a bag?" she asked.
Riley shook his head, picked it up and placed it on my head again. He grinned and took my face in his hands, bringing me closer to him as he lay a gentle kiss on my nose.
"Thank you," he said to the assistant, as he released me and took my hand in his. I just couldn't get over his complete change of attitude.
We walked to Newport Aquarium, paid to get in then began exploring.
"Yeah, he just took it and paid for it," I explained to Steph, as the boys walked on ahead. She smiled and linked arms with me.
"It does make you look extra cute," she said, tugging on it. "You've got him hook, line and sinker."
"But somehow, it just doesn't feel right," I complained.

"I don't understand," Steph said, to which I nodded in agreement then shrugged.
"Me neither. I've spent the whole week flirting with him and trying to understand what's going on between us and now I think I do, I *still* don't get it."
"You're making no sense at all," Steph smiled kindly and I sighed.
"I guess it's nice. Okay, it's *really* nice that he's paying me so much attention and getting all cute with me, but..."
As if on queue, he turned around and gave us a cute wave. As soon as he turned back round, I exploded, but quietly.
"Of course! That's exactly it! Did you just see that?" I said, not pausing to hear her answer. "It was so much more fun when I *didn't* have him. Because that's not the Riley I know, giving us cute waves like a smitten puppy dog. He's brooding, mysterious, sexy..."
Steph rolled her eyes but smiled.
"Unbelievable. He's falling for you and you want him to be toxic boy all over again. There's just no pleasing some people."
I watched Riley ahead of me as she spoke and I just wanted to dramatically slap my own forehead. I needed someone to shock me back to reality; I was clearly going insane.
A little later on, I was walking with Riley. We were looking at these huge sharks swimming around us and over our heads as we walked along a tunnel. It was awe-inspiring and even a little intimidating. And to top it all off, he was back to his normal, sexy self.
"I really love you in that...that..." he said, to which

I filled,
"Hat?"
"No, skimpy bikini."
My jaw dropped then spread into a smile. I slipped my arms around him and snuggled against his chest.
"Now there's the Riley we all know and love."
"You love me being smutty?" he asked with a bemused smirk. I nodded, but said,
"Only occasionally."
He snuggled me tight to him then we released each other and walked hand in hand, pointing to all the sharks and fish swimming carefree around us. We looked at all the other areas, including jellyfish, seahorses and urchins. The last place we went to was The Bizarre and the Beautiful. Riley casually leaned in close to my ear and whispered,
"Do you wanna find a comfy cupboard somewhere so we can get up close and personal?"
I looked around at him, only to find him seductively biting on his lip with one eyebrow raised. My heart raced.
"You'd better be kidding around..."
He shook his head slowly, same facial expression. I rolled my eyes then walked away, as he scurried after me.
"You are just impossible to please, my little butterfly friend."
I looked up at him.
"Do you honestly think so?" I asked seriously. He looked down at me and smiled gently.
"Yeah, I do. You expect a lot from me, but sometimes I just don't know exactly what it is you really *want* from me."

He was so right, and I instinctively wrapped my arm around him and snuggled into his chest.
"I'm sorry. I must be a total nightmare to be with," I said, looking up at him.
He stared down at me for longer than usual.
"You know," he said, his voice deep and breathy in his throat, "you could always just *tell* me what you want."
I leaned away a little, my arms still around his waist, and looked up at him. My heart pounding, I opened my mouth to speak.
"Isn't it obvious?"
"I need to hear it," he whispered back, his eyes burning into mine. This was it. I knew it was all down to me. Whatever I said now would change everything. As I gazed up into his deep chocolate brown eyes, it wasn't even a decision.
"I want...*you*."
As I waited for a reaction, any reaction, I saw his face soften then come towards mine. At the very last moment, I closed my eyes and felt his lips on mine. It was a tender kiss, not rushed or needy. I melted from it as he cupped my face with his hands, and I brought my own up to finally touch that ruffle-able hair. Then he pulled away.
"Well, about time..." he purred gently, before nuzzling my nose and kissing me again. My head was reeling from his words, his smell, his kiss, his touch. As I placed my hands on his waist, I suddenly remembered where we were sharing this make-up kiss…in a public aquarium. I gently pulled away and smiled then looked around us. A few people were watching, then looked away when they realised they'd been rumbled. Riley took his

hands away from my face and I dropped mine too. He took my hand in his and smiled in a way that made me appreciate how totally beautiful he was.
"That comfy cupboard is a-calling," he smirked, as he tugged us out of the room and into the light.
Freddie and Steph were waiting for us on a hexagon shaped bench outside, shaded by the tree that grew out of the middle of it. They smiled as they saw us approach.
"Hey guys. Did you see anything interesting in there?" Freddie asked.
I looked up at Riley, and we both grinned to the point of breaking into giggles.
"I think a few other people might have," I said with a grin. Freddie and Steph smiled and leaned forward.
"What happened?" she asked, with genuine interest. I looked to Riley, who looked to me to answer. Eventually he smiled.
"Oh, you guys wouldn't get it. You'd have to have been there to see it."
I looked up at him as he smiled down at me. I wondered why he'd said that and not 'we kissed' or 'we got back together', but as I wondered what *I* might have said, I realised it wouldn't have been either of those two. They seemed so certain, so definite. The truth was yeah, we'd kissed…but I don't think either of us knew what that meant, or how it changed our relationship. Were we just going to pick up where we left off? I feared the tricky stuff was yet to come as we discussed what we wanted to happen next.
But thankfully, those questions didn't need to be answered at that precise moment. Instead, we all

walked to Eden Park, grabbing some picnic-style food from a grocery store on the way. After a little stroll, we settled down underneath the shade of some trees and had lunch.
"Let's go for a swim in that pool over there," Freddie pointed, as Steph and I sat down.
"You guys go. We'll join you later," Steph said, reading my mind. As Riley peeled off his top in front of me, for some reason, I averted my eyes.
"You sure you don't want to come?" he asked and I shook my head, then looked up at him. God, he's easy on the eyes.
"Nah, we'll come later. I promise."
He smiled and headed off after Freddie.
"So," Steph said inquisitively, as we rolled over onto our fronts and looked out across the park, "what really happened?"
"What? I simply don't know what you're referring to…" I smirked, as she rolled her eyes.
"Tell me now. I can tell it's huge by the look in your eyes."
I smiled widely.
"Riley kissed me."
"About time."
I wide-eyed her at the deja-vu of her statement, then shook my head with a smile.
"So go on. Tell me all…"
I recounted the story, from the comfy cupboard to the kiss. Steph giggled at the end and leaned over to give me a squeeze.
"So what's going to happen next in this little saga?"
I shrugged and looked towards the pool, as if it was going to offer me an answer.
"Who knows? I mean, I feel good about the whole

thing," I smiled with a shrug. "But we still have yet to have that conversation. And things didn't exactly turn out all that great last time around."
"Do you want to be with him?"
"Of course," I replied, squinting in the sun. "But who knows what he's thinking."
Steph grabbed my hand and pulled me to my feet.
"Well let's go find out!" she grinned.
"Wait! What about all our stuff?"
We scooped everything up in a pile and carried it over towards the pool, finishing with a charge and a squeal as we took up speed downhill.
"The party has arrived!" Steph announced, flinging down our stuff. We walked hand in hand to the side of the pool and swung our legs in. It was very, very cold.
"Oh my God!" Steph exclaimed, as we wide-eyed each other and laughed. Riley swam towards me and held onto my legs.
"You'll get used to it," he said convincingly. "But you have to get in first!"
And with that, he wrapped his arms around me tightly and pulled me into the water. I held in a scream but wide-eyed him as I shivered.
"That was low, Mr Kitson."
"Don't be mad, Miss Russo," he pouted, an inch or so from my face. Then he kissed me and all was forgiven. I wrapped my arms and legs around him as we bobbed up and down in the water. All of a sudden, he ducked us both right under the surface then back up again. Spluttering and blinking the water out of my eyes, I pushed away from him and stood alone. He turned and swam towards me with a smile, gilding through the water.

"You're unbelievable," I smiled, as he wrapped his arms around my waist and our slick bodies pressed against each other.
"I'm pretty sure that's my line," he purred, and I closed the gap between us with another kiss. When we broke apart, Freddie was right beside us. I laughed as he wrapped his arms around us both and pulled us into him.
"Ah, you *guys*..." he cooed, before laughing and releasing us. Riley and I swam to the side where Steph was, just watching us with a smile.
We spent about an hour in there, splashing around and swimming. I kept wrapping myself around Riley, but it goes in slow motion because of the drag of the water. It kind of made the whole thing more sensual and romantic, dream-like I guess. We kissed and kissed, like we'd been released from somewhere that had forbidden us to do it. I remembered how good it felt and he obviously felt the same as his hands wandered all over me, as well as his kisses.
When we finally crawled out, we were starving hungry and tired. We dried off in the sun as we finished off our picnic food, then settled down to enjoy the last of the afternoon sunshine. Steph was lying on her front, Freddie on his back. Riley was lying with his head on my tummy, as I gently stroked his hair. It was blissful, especially when the warm breeze blew over us.
None of us wanted to move, but eventually we packed up and headed back to the motorhome. When we got there, the clouds had gone grey and the temperature had dropped considerably. I changed into a t-shirt and swiped Riley's hoody off

the end of the bed.
"May I…?" I asked, as I slipped it on.
He grabbed a handful of the front and tugged me towards him.
"Of course," he said, kissing me as I wrapped my arms around his neck and pulled him closer to me. As we pulled apart, he snuggled into me for a hug and briefly lifted me off my feet.
"Riley?"
"Yes, butterfly?" he said, as he set me down again.
"This is going to sound ridiculous probably, but…did that kiss mean we're back together?"
He looked at me as if I was stupid and replied, "Of course not."
My heart sunk and it must have shown in my face because he pulled me onto the bed with him and kissed my neck.
"I'm just teasing. I think it did if you think it did."
He rolled away from me as I wriggled onto my side and rubbed his tummy.
"I think it did," I said, bringing my face up to his.
"Then it did," he replied, kissing me again.
A few moments later, I climbed up to sit straddled on top of him.
"Riley?"
He smiled, rolling his eyes.
"Yes, butterfly?"
He slid his fingers into mine, our hands clasped between us palm to palm, as we gently pushed against each other, our hands moving back and forth.
"Why did you wait so long to kiss me back?"
"Honestly?" he asked, quirking an eyebrow at me.
I nodded.

“I didn’t know if you really wanted to get back together,” he said.
I arched an eyebrow at him.
“Did you miss all those signals I was hurling at you this week?”
“Oh no, I got them,” he nodded. “They were just a pretty mixed bag, is all.”
“*I* was sending mixed messages?” I retorted, arching my eyebrow higher still. Riley smiled and shrugged his shoulders.
“I just wanted to be sure this time, you know?”
I gazed down at him and nodded.
“I really do want this to work this time,” he said sincerely, gazing back up at me. I smiled and pushed his hands apart so I could lean right down and hover my face just an inch from his.
“Me too,” I smiled, before closing my eyes and sealing my statement with a kiss.

***

By the time we set off that night, it was cold, dark and windy.
"That’s certainly a quick change in weather," Steph said, as we pulled out of the trailer park and headed towards the 71 Interstate. I snuggled into Riley, my feet tucked up between me and Steph. He kissed my forehead as I happily closed my eyes and rested against him. It felt so nice, I easily fell asleep.
When I woke up again, we'd stopped.
"Are we in Nashville?" Steph asked, as she sat up, allowing me to finally stretch out my legs. Freddie nodded.

"Yep. I am officially king of the road."
"You really are, baby," Steph said, kissing him heartily on the cheek. I sat up as Riley yawned and stretched his arms above his head, then let them slowly fall behind me.
"Let's go to bed. I'm exhausted," he said, opening the door and climbing out. I followed and we stood in the cool night air waiting for Freddie to unlock the door. I was so glad to be in Riley's hoody.
As we crawled into bed, I snuggled up to him as he looked down at me with sleepy eyes.
"It feels so good to have you again."
My heart warmed as I stretched up and kissed his forehead.
"I know exactly what you mean," I said, as I snuggled into him and closed my eyes.

I wanted to ask him if he thought we could really make it work this time. Or rather, *how* we would make it work. Had anything really changed these last few months, except my zip code? But I knew too well that if I spoke, I might spoil it. Time would tell with this one, but right now, I just had to follow my heart.

JULY 28th

Tennessee was everything I'd hoped for and more. We started in Nashville, where we spent the day on the General Jackson Showboat, cruising carefree down the Cumberland River. But it was at night when the place really came to life. We'd been recommended to visit The District by Caleb Tanner, our old high school pal turned Harmony boyband superstar, who originally hailed from Nashville. He wasn't wrong. The District was incredible. Wandering from one honky-tonk bar to the next, drinking Lynchburg Lemonades and eating ribs smothered in Jack Daniel's sticky sauce, we thought we'd died and gone to Southern Heaven. The whole place was steeped in this cool, laidback vibe, which suited us down to the ground and made for a very low-down and dirty backdrop against which Riley and I could play out the beginning of our back-on-track relationship. To the strains of some seriously grimy country music, Riley and I made out like there was no tomorrow. Like no one knew who we were. They probably did, of course – it's not like they don't get cable out here – but at the same time, no one seemed to care. No one bothered us, asked for our autographs, or even so much as looked our way. I finally felt like we were on vacation and I could truly relax.

***

From Nashville (after sleeping off some serious hangovers), we made our way onto our final destination of the road-trip - Memphis.
"I can't believe it's almost over," I pouted, as we watched the sign flash by on the highway. Riley, who had his arm around me, gave me a squeeze and kissed my cheek.
"Maybe we could just go on and drive forever."
"Oh, don't tease me," I sighed. "I would absolutely sign up for that."
"Me too," Steph said. "Going back to work, to LA, is the last thing I feel like doing."
"Hey!" Freddie interjected.
"Oh baby, not like that. I can't wait to get back home and stretch out in our bed."
"Actually, that would be pretty nice," I agreed, thinking about my cool, crisp sheets back home. Our motorhome sheets hadn't been changed since New York – gross.
"It's just, once we go home, I mean, that's it. Back to reality."
"Back to work," Riley added.
"Back to normality," I grumbled.

"Ugh, normality sucks," Steph groaned.
"Screw normality!" Riley declared. "Let's just fill up the tank and keep driving. What's the next state?"
"Um, Arkansas, I think," Freddie mused. Riley frowned as he paused, deep in thought.
"Well, um... okay, then. Arkansas it is. Go Arkansas!"
Steph and I whooped for Arkansas, which just sounded wrong.
"Then it's Oklahoma," Freddie said.
"Oklahoma!" we all chorused, before laughing. We named all the states, through Texas, New Mexico, Arizona and finally, California, before collapsing with a sigh. I snuggled into Riley and smiled.
"It doesn't matter where we go," he whispered in my ear, "so long as we're together."
I grinned and closed my eyes as I lay my head to rest on his shoulder. He wasn't wrong about that.

***

Of course we went to Graceland - how could we not? Riley had us all in stitches with his Elvis impression, which he proceeded to do every time our tour guide turned her back. She must have thought we were so rude, sniggering our way round the tour, but we just couldn't help ourselves. He was hilarious. But it was impossible not to fall serious at times, given the history of the place. By the time we made our way into the Meditation Garden, I think all our thoughts had turned towards the sanctity of life and just how much we ought to make the most of it. I gazed at Riley when he was deep in thought, staring across the garden, and wondered if he was going to be my one true love. Right now, I felt so close to him, so into him. Would we live out our lives together? Sit out back in our own private garden someday, watching the world go by, side by side? He looked down at me, locked his eyes with mine and smiled. In that moment, I sure hoped so.

But for now, I was content with having a funny, spontaneous and easy-on-the-eyes companion to have fun with. He piggybacked me all along the Memphis Walk of Fame before we stopped for ice-creams, then chased me all around Robert R. Church Park playing tag with Steph and Freddie. The four of us were just big kids really, determined never to grow up and get bored. I think the time spent at Graceland had made us think seriously about the future, and in reaction to that, we'd decided to hell with it - we were going to live squarely in the moment and enjoy it.

We sat and watched the sun go down, feeling the temperature drop. I sat between Riley's legs, my back to his chest, as he wrapped his arms and the sides of his hooded zip sweatshirt around me for warmth.

There was so much we could have said to each other. Instead, we said nothing, listening to the sound of the blues drifting across the park from a nearby bar. If that wasn't a near-perfect moment in time, then I don't know that there ever will be.

***

We dropped the motorhome back at their Memphis depot the next day. Standing by the side of the road

with our luggage, we looked a miserable sight. Freddie stuck out his arm and hailed a cab.
"The flight's at noon, right?" Steph asked.
"Just after. Quarter past," I confirmed with a nod.
"So we'll meet you there?"
"Absolutely," I nodded. "We'll get the next one."
We all helped load Steph and Freddie's stuff into the back of the cab.
"We'll see you at the airport then in, what, half an hour?" Freddie said, as Steph climbed in.
"Something like that," Riley said, and Freddie gave us a wave before climbing in and shutting the door.
I watched as the car pulled into the traffic and disappeared up the road.
I felt a pair of hands slide around my waist and a pair of arms cuddle me from behind.
"Don't feel blue," Riley said, resting his chin on my shoulder.
"We're in the home of the blues," I joked flatly. "It only seems fitting."
"Hey."
Riley pulled away from me briskly and I turned to face him with a frown.
"Snap out of it," he said, pointing a finger at me.
"I...uh..." I started, but instead, he smiled.
"Where do you think I'm going when we get back to New York?"
"I don't know. Home?" I shrugged.
"And that'll be what, a forty minute drive from yours?"
I squinted in the sunshine, raising my hand to shield my eyes.
"Yeah, I guess..."
Riley smiled the most charming of smiles.

"Do you really think this is the last you're going to see of me this summer?"
His smile must have been contagious because a hint of one played on my own lips.
"No..."
"Girl, you're going to be sick of me by the time the summer ends."
"No I won't!" I declared, skipping the few steps between us and throwing my arms around his neck. He lifted me off the ground and spun me round, placing me back down on the floor with a kiss.
"I hate to get all Danny Zuko on you, but what's that line? On the beach at the beginning?"
I paused, my mind kick-starting into life, trying desperately to remember... I smiled, from ear to ear, then composed myself with a flick of the hair.
"Riley, is this the end?" I asked, gazing up adoringly into his eyes.
"Of course not," he replied. "It's only the beginning."
Then we jumped apart and started singing the opening beats of the song to each other before grinning at each other.
"Come on," he said, holding out his arm to hail a cab. I reached down and picked up my bags with renewed enthusiasm. Going home wasn't such a bad thing. I would get to see Evan, sleep in my own bed, have a shower that wasn't run off a pump...
And taking Riley home with me, this time as my boyfriend, was the very best souvenir of all.

SEPTEMBER 2nd

Going back to Davey's Crowd felt a little strange this time around. For a start, I can't believe we're on season four already. I don't think any of us expected the show to do so well, or be so popular, certainly not year after year. Plus we were all returning with a movie under our belt (except Connor - he was shooting his first, a Western of all things, over the Christmas vacation), and that had certainly changed things. As friends, we were the same, albeit a little shaky to get off the ground and become reacquainted after the summer break. But as actors, certainly, we'd all upped our game. When I got a chance to stand back and watch the others between takes, I was amazed at how much we'd all improved. Not obviously, but in subtle ways. It was in a look, or a gesture, a tone of voice that just sounded that little bit more genuine. We were all saying our lines as though they came from us, from the heart, and not from off the page. I was proud of

the guys and of course, myself. I'd been right to take the role of Jessica Albright because, quite unexpectedly, it had benefited Casey Bridges too. The writers were well aware of it being our fourth season, and they had the unenviable challenge of moving the action on to college. For us, that meant shooting exteriors at the nearby Northeastern University, but other than that, we were still largely based in Lexington. It was fun exploring our new campus dormitory sets, like getting to play out the 'going away to college' scenario for real. Despite my disastrous, and brief, foray into further education, I was excited at getting to play act the experience. In the most clichéd of ways, all five principal cast members were going to the same school, with Casey and Regan in one dorm, Davey, Jonny and Ethan in another. I mean, as if! But whatever, the fans didn't care, so long as we were all there. Audience feedback from season three had ultimately been disappointed at Casey and Jonny's break-up, so the writers had Josh and I hooking up again by the end of the season. But for now, at least until the end of the year, we were back in bitchy banter territory. That suited me fine, because it meant I didn't have any hot and heavy scenes to film, no heart-breaking emotional confessions - put another way, no opportunities to have Josh or I start questioning the nature of our own relationship. I didn't need another 'life imitating art imitating life' kind of season.
Not that it would have played out like that anyway, I suppose. Josh was still happily loved up with Lori (they'd just celebrated five months together, can you believe it?) and I was in the re-

honeymoon phase of my relationship with Riley. Following the road trip, it had been a case of spending half our time on the East Coast and half our time on the West Coast, where he'd bought his first place, a gorgeous condo in Studio City. I'd had the best summer ever. Strolls through Central Park, sunbathing on Long Beach, shopping on Fifth Avenue, brunch on Melrose - we were living the all-American loved-up dream.

Sadly, that dream came to end when our Fall schedules landed on our doormats. He started back on Hazy Days on September 1st, me on September 2nd. We spent our last night together at his apartment in Manhattan, cuddled up on the balcony under his thick fur blanket.

"I don't know how I'm going to get out of bed in the morning without you being beside me," he drawled, his breath warm on the back of my neck, his arms wrapped tightly around me as I lay back against his chest.

"Actually," he said, "I'm amazed I ever got *out* of bed this summer, with you being all gorgeous and naked in it."

He nuzzled into my neck, making me giggle.

"I've had the best time with you," I sighed contentedly.

There was a quiet moment of contemplation, a highlights package running through both our minds.

"Me too," he finally replied.

"We're just going to have to make even more effort to see each other, that's all," I said hopefully.

It fell quiet between us again. Was he as worried as me that out of sight might mean out of mind? Or

would absence make the heart grow fonder, as I hoped? I decided to stop worrying about it and I snuggled into his embrace, determined to make those last few hours together count.
I also knew that although I didn't necessarily have more important things to worry about, I did have other things to worry about generally. After several months of post-production, it was almost time to promote Irresponsible Actions. Trish had been inundated with calls lining up interviews and photo shoots and press tours. But I was more concerned about my leading man. I sincerely hoped my relationship with Oliver was one that hadn't changed at all, and we could just take up right where we left off - as friends. All I wanted to do was promote the movie and have it be a big, fat success. If I could do that with Oliver on one arm and Riley on the other then hell, all my dreams would have come true at once.

OCTOBER 8th

I'd heard from a few of my friends, and some well-versed family members, that doing movie promotion was a tiresome exercise, so I thought I was pretty well-prepared. I was wrong. Irresponsible Actions secured a worldwide release, which was super exciting, and Young Bros. were keen to get Oliver and I out to promote it as much as possible. But I almost choked on my smoothie when Trish showed me the schedule.

"I know it looks a lot," she said, running her hand down a page full of squiggles, dates, and times. "But it'll be fine."

"And when am I supposed to sleep in the next two weeks?" I joked half-heartedly.

"On the plane," came the serious reply, and I stared hard at the diary. Oh well. If this is what movie stars had to do, then I was just going to have to embrace it. And besides, I had Oliver (and even occasionally, Jess) to keep me company. How hard could it be?

***

Very, as it turned out. We flew to Manhattan to start with early morning talk shows, a few mid-afternoon shows, and several magazine interviews for overseas publications. Back to back, it seemed pretty busy, and I soon noticed a pattern emerging in the questions. The same things were being asked over and over again, it seemed - how did you and Oliver get along? What was it like making your first big movie? Oh, and how are things between you and Riley? I hadn't been expecting that - I had my professional promoting head on - but without fail, they asked about my private life, and each time, I had to politely and carefully deflect revealing too much. With a smile and a polite nod of the head, I'd assure them everything was fine, and they would have no choice but to move on. This pattern of questioning soon became a *joke*. By the time we'd done the East Coast (New York, Boston, down to Washington and finally, Miami), I felt like I was starting to lose my mind.
"Is it just me, or are we being asked the same questions over and over...?" I asked Oliver, as we sat in the departure lounge at yet another airport. I'd been stupid to worry about us - we'd picked up exactly where we'd left off, no awkwardness at all.
"Tell me about it," he said, running his hand through his curls. "It's like that movie, the one where they get stuck living the same day over and over..."

"Groundhog Day?" I suggested and he nodded.
"That's it. It's like, 'Come on guys. Try and be little original, please'."
I nodded and sighed.
"I feel like I'm losing my mind."
On the plus side, being asked the same questions meant giving out the same answers. I could pretty much be on auto-pilot (which was helpful on little-to-no sleep). But then Trish stung me a few days in and told me I couldn't do that, as everything printed would be the same, and the magazines would get sniffy that they didn't have anything 'exclusive'.
"Just try and you know, change it up every so often," she suggested.
That proved harder than it sounded. There's only a few ways to answer *exactly* the same question and just as I thought I was getting the hang of it, I found myself stumbling over my words and leaving great big pauses as my mind tried to act like a spongy human thesaurus.
"You're trying too hard to be original," Trish commented, as we left the Sunrise studios in Los Angeles at just after 8am. I rolled my eyes out of sight. I couldn't win!
"You know something?" I said to Oliver, yawning as I lay my head to rest on his shoulder in the back of a blacked-out car. "I'll be glad when this is all over."
Oliver put his arm around me and gave me a squeeze.
"As I much as I love you, Beccy, I can't wait to get rid of you either."
I smiled and gave him a playful nudge in the ribs.

At least we had each other.

***

My final engagement was on The Joey Cruz show. I was dreading it. After January's debacle, I wasn't looking forward to a re-match. Only last week, Kerry Talby had actually stormed off the set mid-interview after he asked about her divorce from her husband.

It turned out I needn't have worried. Sure, he gently ribbed Oliver and I about our 'chemistry', but he was playing things really cautiously. Perhaps he'd been burned by the Kerry experience.

"Well, you really are a rising star, Rebecca Russo," Joey charmed, wholly unlike the version I'd met earlier on in the year. "Season four of Davey's Crowd and a brand new movie to promote. And am I right in saying that things are going pretty well personally for you too? You're back with Riley Kitson?"

I smiled and nodded in affirmation.

"Yes, that's right."

Cue the hearty audience applause, plus a few cheap wolf-whistles.

"And things are going well?"

"They are."

Joey looked to Oliver.

"And how do you feel about this, buddy? I mean, you've played opposite Rebecca now, you've got to know her... Is she a catch?"

Oliver nodded.

"She sure is."

"Aww," I smiled at him, patting his arm.

"And you're not just the least bit jealous that it's not you that'll be walking her up the red carpet next week for the premiere of Irresponsible Actions?" Joey pushed.
Oliver paused before brushing his hand down the front of his shirt. He shifted a little in his chair. He looked kind of...awkward, I suppose.
"I mean, look at her," he said, holding his hand towards me but avoiding my gaze. "Who wouldn't? But it's not meant to be."
I furrowed my brow in confusion. Was this really the time to get serious about the status - or lack thereof - of our relationship?
"Well, it sure would boost the ratings," Joey summised, tapping his fingers on the desk in front of him. "Not that you need it of course. This movie's going to be a commercial hit, I'm sure."
I looked from Oliver back to Joey and smiled.
"We sure hope so. We put a lot of hard work into it. We really believe in it."
Joey nodded.
"I mean, let's not get ahead of ourselves," he said, holding his hand out at me. "I don't think we'll be placing bets on any Oscar nominations, *but...*"
The audience laughed and I felt hurt. He was probably right - this was a teen movie after all - but there was no need to be so dismissive. We certainly didn't need Mr Judgemental putting negative thoughts into the minds of movie-goers before the damn movie had even been released.
"It's not all about the critics," Oliver piped up. "It's about the fans."
He pointed at the audience, who whooped and squealed as they had done every time he'd

addressed them, and I grinned proudly. What a way to bring it back around.
"Well, good luck with the movie," Joey said, clearly knowing he was defeated. "And if you guys out there want to check it out, Irresponsible Actions opens next Friday at theatres across the country."
The audience applauded, the lights dimmed and the floor manager counted us out into the commercial break. Joey stood up to shake our hands then Oliver and I crossed the stage towards the exit. I didn't know quite what to say to him. Should I ask him about what he'd said, I wondered, or just leave it be? Before I had a chance to decide, Trish came rushing towards us.
"The early figures say the show just got its season highest ratings!"
"What, *this* show?" Oliver thumbed behind him.
"You two are the talk of the town!" she enthused.
Oliver raised his eyebrows and glanced at me. I held his gaze and smiled gently.
"Well, come *on*," he said with a cheeky grin, wrapping his arms around me and squeezing me tightly into him. "I'd be disappointed if we weren't. Look at us!"
I giggled and Trish put her hand on her hip.
"If you keep this up, you'll open the box office at number one next week, I'm telling you."
My heart fluttered as Oliver released me. He wide-eyed me and clapped his hands together.
"Now that's what I'm talking about!"

OCTOBER 13th

Trish sure had pulled some strings to get me in this Benicio Borma dress. I looked down at the floral design, big red flowers printed on cream silk, and ran my fingers down the smooth material. It was a head-turner, for sure, and exactly what I'd wanted. Trish had tentatively asked if I'd wanted to go down the 'Stars and Hype' route, which meant in agent-speak, 'Do you want a dress the size of a handkerchief again?'. I'd had fun pushing the limits last year but I felt differently about this event. This was my first big movie premiere, the first time I had my name in lights and on billboards, the first time all eyes would be on me...and I wanted to make it count. The movie had a serious tone, and I wanted to be seen as a mature, bankable actress, so I needed a look to match. We'd been sent a whole bunch of dresses, which were beautiful, but they'd been by little-known (or in some cases, unknown)

designers. It was Trish who'd said aloud what I'd been thinking.
"You know, I think I'm going to put in a few calls to some bigger names," she mused. "I think we need to aim a little higher on this one."
She took one look at my wide, eager eyes and raised her hand.
"Calm down, Beccy. I can't promise anything."
"I know, I know..." I nodded, lowering my gaze.
"But there's no harm in asking," she concluded, reaching for the phone.
Three days later, she called me to announce that none other than Benicio Borma had sent me a dress from his Spring collection. I couldn't believe my luck!
"Is it pretty?" I asked excitedly.
"Honey, it's to die for. Seriously."
"Then I don't even need to see it," I declared. "*That's* the one I'm going to wear."
Of course, I'd had to go in for a fitting, but wow, even in my wildest dreams I hadn't expected it to be so striking. Being made of silk helped it to flow and swish and I whirled around in circles, watching it fan gently around me.
"I feel..." I began with a dreamy sigh. Trish smiled back at me in confirmation.
"You look even better."
Now here we were, minutes from the red carpet for my first movie premiere, in the back of a limousine, wearing a Benicio Borma dress. This must be what making it feels like, I thought with a secret smile.
"Okay, so don't forget, you *have* to name drop Benicio..." Trish said, turning towards me.
I nodded.

"Of course."
"And try to keep things on the movie, okay? It's going to be hard, but that's what you're here for."
"Of course," I frowned, shrugging my shoulders. "What else would I be talking about?"
Riley, apparently. It seemed completely unfair that after having decided *not* to use the premiere for our first big public appearance in favour of keeping the focus on Irresponsible Actions that no one seemed to care anyway. Every interview on the red carpet started with the question, 'So where's Riley?'. Clearly that was all they cared about, my celebrity couple status, and not about the movie at all. I tried to keep a light-hearted and positive outlook on things but eight interviews later, I was waning.
"Trish, this is so unfair," I complained, as she pointed across the carpet at yet another interviewer.
"What is?" she asked, distracted.
"All they keep asking about is Riley."
She looked at me.
"Well, what did you expect?"
I'd naively expected them to ask me about the movie-making process, how I'd 'found' my character, what techniques I'd employed to make Jessica Albright believable and likeable, but no. They just wanted to know who was taking me to bed at night. I lifted my dress off the floor and strode across the carpet with my shoulders back and my head held high. I plastered a smile on my face but inside, I felt like crying. So much for making it.
Once inside, things turned a little more serious and as the credits rolled, and the principal cast and

crew were invited to the front of the auditorium for a round of applause and a brief Q & A, I started to feel worthy again. Finally, I was being asked questions about 'the craft', how I thought the movie would play to my Davey's Crowd fans, how we'd managed to achieve an independent tone to an otherwise big studio movie. Jess squeezed my hand as we drowned in a round of final applause and grinned at me,
"Let's get druuuunk!"
Oh yeah, the after-party. Now, *that* was fun. I kicked off my expensive but painful shoes, hitched up my Benicio Borma dress and got down to some serious dirty dancing with Oliver. We even had a private DJ set by DJ Dreem, which was out of this world! And as for the getting drunk part, we could only get drunk on love and laughter – alcohol was strictly off-limits for us under-age actors at this public event. Although some creepy executive producer did offer to buy me a glass of champagne to 'celebrate' but the way he asked, I felt like I'd be selling my soul to him if I'd accepted. But I didn't really need the alcohol anyway. Around Oliver, my inhibitions were always a little lowered, and with the music pumping from the speakers, the disco lights lighting us up, and two of my best friends by my side, I was on top of the world.
The only thing missing was a partner for the last dance, a strong pair of arms wrapped around me and a kiss that told me I was loved. Instead, I had to make do with a late-night phone call to Riley out on the smoker's balcony.
"How did it go?" he asked.
"Okay, I suppose," I shrugged to myself.

"Why, what happened?"
"It was all about you, funnily enough."
"*Me*?" he asked, incredulously.
"Everyone wanted to know why you weren't there. They barely even asked me about the movie."
There was a pause, then a heavy, frustrated sigh.
"Son of a – I'm sorry, Beccy."
"I wouldn't have minded if you'd actually been here. I would have expected the spotlight to be on us. I don't know..." I sighed, "I just hoped that, you know, this was my chance to be the centre of attention for my work, not for my celebrity status."
"You just can't win with these people," Riley offered and I nodded.
"Hey, look," he said. "It's not like this is going to be your last red carpet. Or premiere, for that matter. You're gonna make a ton of movies and win a ton of awards and the last thing they'll be asking you about is me."
I grinned and let out a little giggle.
"You really think so?"
"I know so. You're gonna be a superstar...and you'll have traded me in for some newer model, anyway."
I gasped.
"No, I won't."
"I'll bet you will."
"Don't talk crap," I said with a smile, picturing his handsome face in my mind. "I think you and I are gonna walk that red carpet together a few more times yet."
"Anyway, I'll let you get back to your after-party, *superstar*."
I rolled my eyes and smiled.

"I'm going to see you soon, right?"
"Sure."
I didn't know when, and neither did he, so for now, that had to be enough.
"Thanks for the support."
"Anytime, butterfly."
We said goodbye and I stared at the phone.
"I *thought* you were out here," Jess said, appearing at my side. I stood up and put my phone in my bag.
"Oh God, you weren't mooning to your *boy*-friend, were you? 'Oh sweetie, I miss you'. 'I miss you morrre'..."
I pulled an unimpressed face and she laughed.
"Come on," she said, reaching for my hand and leading me to the door. "You only get one 'first movie' after-party and this is it."
She was right. But more than that, I hoped Riley was right, and that I'd have a few more after-parties to come after this. I'd had just a taste of what it was like to be an A-Lister, and I already knew I wanted more.

NOVEMBER 23rd

I noticed the paparazzi just before we pulled up alongside the sidewalk. I glanced at Riley, who had spotted them too. He ran his fingers through his hair then arched an eyebrow at me.
"I wonder how they found out," I mused.
He reached across and took hold of my hand.
"It doesn't matter. They can sit across the table from us for all I care..."
He raised my hand to his lips and kissed my curled fingers, his deep brown eyes locked onto mine as they peered over the top.
"I finally get to spend the night with my girl."
I grinned and leaned towards him as he lowered our hands and I closed my eyes to savour a sweet kiss... But the door opened, and I turned to see the sidewalk fill with jostling bodies and flashing camera bulbs. With a sigh, I turned my body to shuffle across the seat and get out of the car, but

Riley kept hold of my hand and pulled me back to him with a tug, our lips colliding.
"I couldn't have made it through the whole evening without that," he grinned at me and I grinned back before finally climbing out of the car. I'd worn loose fitting trousers instead of a dress so I didn't have to worry about doing it too gracefully. Instead I pushed my hair behind my ears before shoving my fingers into my pockets. It was a very cold November night.
Riley rose out of the car to stand beside me in a flood of bright white light. He slammed the door shut behind us then placed a commanding hand on my back, leading us towards the main doors of the restaurant. The paparazzi followed us, calling our names, begging for us to turn around and pose, but we ignored them, and found ourselves in the warm sanctuary of The Olive Garden.
"Good evening," the maitre'd said charmingly. "May I take your coats?"
Riley helped me off with mine first, revealing a pretty pink (and pretty see-through) blouse with a ruffled neck and billowing sleeves. He paused to look me over and smiled, before taking off his own coat. He'd opted for a white shirt, under a black waistcoat, sleeves rolled up. As he ran his hand through his hair, it was my turn to gaze upon him and smile.
"Come on," he said. "I see them."
Steering me through the tables, his hand once again on my back, I scanned the restaurant and saw a long table only about half-full. Steph stood up, unable to help herself, and hurried between the other tables towards us.

"Oh my God, Bec-cy!" she beamed, throwing her arms around me. I held her tightly in an embrace and closed my eyes. Oh, it had been way too long.
"I've missed you!" she enthused and I nodded as she pulled away.
"I've missed you too," I said, reaching up to touch her hair. "And look at you! This is nice."
Her hair was cut a lot shorter than usual, just below her shoulders, in a sleek bob.
"I know," she said, reaching up to touch it herself. "It was for the movie."
"How did that go?"
She nodded brightly.
"Good, yeah. Really good, actually. Anyway, let's get you seated... Hey Riley!"
"I was wondering when you'd notice," he teased, and she rolled her eyes.
"Don't be silly. As if anyone could miss you entering a room."
I watched as they hugged each other and I smiled warmly up at him.
"Come this way," Steph beckoned, and we walked behind her, as Freddie got up from his seat to greet us.
"Hey, how's it going?" I asked, wrapping my arms around his neck and giving him a squeeze.
"Yeah, good," he said, patting my back as he released me, but he seemed a little 'off' somehow. With a polite smile, he sat back down and reached for his water. Maybe they'd had a little fight before they got here. I looked down the table and waved at Eli and Evan, who waved back.
"Don't forget, I've got to get you to sign that thing for TiVo," Evan pointed at me. "It's being installed

next week."
"I thought you two lived together?" Steph asked, as I sat down beside her.
"We do. It's just I've been off promoting Irresponsible Actions, so I've hardly been around..."
"Of course!" she grinned. "Congratulations! How did it go?"
"The promotion? Ugh, it was exhausting. I can't believe they ask you the same crap, over and over..."
"No, I meant the opening weekend."
I grinned at Riley, who looked back at me with a proud smile.
"We opened second!" I declared with a grin.
Steph nodded and smiled, clapping her hands together.
"That's amazing!"
"Yeah, well, we would have been first but that new kids movie opened, you know, the one with the talking crabs?"
Steph rolled her eyes.
"Oh, you'll never beat them. I don't know why the studios even bother putting their movies up against the Believe Studios stuff. It's an impossible task."
"Maybe we should look at doing more voice-over work," Riley said, reaching for the carafe to fill up his glass. "That way we can say we opened at number one at the box office."
"That's not a bad idea."
"And when does Scared come out?"
"January 31st next year," Steph smiled excitedly. "They're going for a quiet slot. They figure that way, they've got no competition."

"Yeah, horror movies are usually released around Halloween, right?"
Steph nodded.
"Yeah, sometimes earlier in the Spring too. But January's the dumping ground, so..."
She shrugged and I sensed worry in her.
"How do you think it's going to go?" I asked tentatively. Her face lit up.
"Oh, fine," she said with a nod. "I think it's a good decision. They were aiming for December this year, but they figured they'd wait. No, I think it's going to be amazing, Beccy. You're going to love it!"
"I'm sure I will. Anything Karl puts his name to is usually great."
"How modest of you," Steph smiled, and I smiled back. There was a part of me that had hoped when Karl wrote his first big-screen horror movie that he might have asked me to be in it. But I knew Steph had the dark, occult Vampire High success going for her, and it was an easier, more believable transition. It couldn't have been further from Davey's Crowd. I reminded myself that my own movie had just opened mega-successfully, and that if and when Karl wrote another one, he was sure to throw a cameo my way. Well, he'd better...
"Hey everyone!"
We all turned to see Jenna striding towards us, holding the hand of a bashful looking Jesse Kane. I loved his music - hell, most of middle America did - but I was surprised to see him here, at our Thanksgiving dinner.
"Guys, this is Jesse. Jesse, this is everyone!" she announced happily, waving her arm along the length of the table. We all raised our hands and

smiled and said 'hi', and Jenna turned to give him an overtly passionate kiss before taking their seats.
"Did you know about this?" I asked, turning to Steph.
"She asked if she could bring a plus one, but..." she replied, raising her shoulders in a shrug. I looked along the table towards Eli. It had been over a year, probably nearly two, since they'd split up, but even so, Jenna's PDA-fest with her new Billboard Hot 100 boyfriend was hardly tactful. Eli, ever the sweetheart, gave them both a polite smile then turned back to his conversation with Evan.
"Steph, hey!" Jenna waved along the table. "How are you?"
"Good, thanks."
As they began talking over us, Riley and I sat back a little in our chairs and looked at each other. He reached his hand over and lay it on my thigh, and I intertwined my fingers with his, stroking the back of his hand dreamily.
"You know," he said, leaning a little closer, "we could just skip straight to dessert..."
I smirked and glanced at him, arching an eyebrow.
"I'm just saying..." he added.
"All in good time," I replied, kissing his nose and making him squint his eyes shut.
Over the next few minutes, the last of the gang arrived, mostly Freddie's friends, like Tim and Mattie. Sadie made her fashionably late entrance, declaring she simply couldn't get away from a meeting that her father (the famous director Scott Simpson) had just taken with up-and-coming Kory Hall. We pretty much all raised our eyebrows in unison, half at the cool factor of meeting Kory, and

half at Sadie bragging about it. She sat down opposite Evan and flashed him a forced smile. "Hi."
"Hi," he replied, and I can't be sure, but I think that's pretty much all they said to each other all night.
We all ordered our food, and the conversation began to flow as easily as the wine (on account of some of our slightly older companions, we'd managed to get around the rest of us being under-age). It was great catching up with everyone, and Riley settled in easily, his charm carrying him some of the way and his hilarious anecdotes the rest. I got a chance to speak to Jesse, and ended up sounding like a gushing super fan.
"I just love 'By The Numbers'," I smiled, my hand over my heart to add to the sincerity. He nodded and smiled back.
"Thanks."
"Really. I listen to it all the time on set."
"Oh," he said, pointing at me, "Davey's Crowd, right? I've seen some of that. I mean, when I'm not on tour and stuff."
"Really?" I asked, eyebrows raised. "That's amazing. I wouldn't have pegged you for a fan."
"Oh, I wouldn't go so far as saying 'fan'..."
"Sure, sure," I said, waving my hand dismissively. "Anyway... So how did you meet Jenna?"
At the mention of her name, she invited herself into the conversation, her arm draped around his shoulder as she leaned in towards me.
"Oh, we met backstage at one of his gigs," she explained.
"And you couldn't have taken me along?"

“You were off doing promotion,” she stated. “And besides, I wouldn't have been much company. I had other things on my mind...”
She lay her hand on his cheek and kissed the one closest to her. He looked a little embarrassed by it all, if I was reading the signals right. Jenna, on the other hand, looked like the cat that had got the cream.
“Well, it's really great to have you here,” I said, changing the subject.
“Thanks for inviting me,” Jesse nodded. “I can see you guys all know each other pretty well.”
“We've been friends for years,” Jenna said, smiling at me.
“Some might say too long.”
“Hey!” she retorted, and I grinned.
“Yeah...” I said, gazing around the group. These were all familiar faces. Although Evan was actual family, they all felt like family to me somehow. I realised I needed to make more time for things like this. Work was work, and that was great and all, but times like these, people like these – that was what life was really all about.
“Don't worry, honey,” Jenna said, nuzzling her nose against Jesse's neck. “You'll be part of the gang in no time.”
I might have been wrong, but as Jenna closed her eyes and smiled smugly, I was pretty sure Jesse made a sly glance towards the exit.
“Oh, Beccy?” Jenna added. “Have you spoken to Oliver recently?”
“Not since the premiere, no. Why?”
She shrugged.
“He told me he was going to be in town this

weekend, is all."
I furrowed my brow a little, glancing at Jesse, who was oblivious.
"Have you guys been in touch then?" I asked curiously.
Jenna nodded brightly.
"Yeah," she replied casually, picking at a manicured fingernail. "I mean, we've been texting and stuff…"
Was she *testing* me? She'd barely looked up to note my reaction, which was currently a deeply furrowed brow and a slightly aghast jaw. What an odd time to drop in that she and Oliver had a relationship I didn't know about. Was it platonic? It had to be - she was practically sitting on Jesse Kane's lap. But why hadn't Oliver mentioned it to me during promotion? Just what was going on between them?
I could probe no further without looking jealous, and besides, the waiters were arriving with our food.
It was all absolutely delicious, but as dessert was cleared, I became distracted by Freddie as he made a move to stand up. A hush descended on the table as he raised his glass.
"I, uh, I just wanted to say a few words..."
"Oh God, here comes the Emmy award-winning speech," Mattie teased, and Tim laughed.
"Hey, at least some of us *have* an Emmy, my friend," Freddie retorted, receiving a round of laughter and applause from the rest of us.
"Anyway, I, uh... I just wanted to thank you all for coming tonight. This being our Thanksgiving dinner and all, I thought it was appropriate to,

uh...say thanks."
I smiled up at him, but pulled a little face to myself when I knew he wasn't looking. Freddie wasn't exactly at home being centre of attention but this speech was bombing.
"Me and Steph, Steph and *I*," he corrected. "Being over in LA..."
"Bragger!" Mattie 'coughed' under his breath, and we all laughed. Freddie looked down at him, focussed his eyes on him, then continued.
"We've really missed seeing you all, although after that remark, I'm thinking maybe we were wrong..."
"Oh, come on," Mattie said, pushing his seat back and getting up, throwing his arms around Freddie dramatically.
"We've missed you too, King."
Freddie patted him on the back but pushed him away, and as Mattie sat back down, he and Tim started talking and joking about something.
"Ah, come on guys, will you let the man speak?" Evan called out.
"Yeah!" Riley clapped, and we all began clapping and urging Freddie to go on. He blushed a little and took a long swig of his wine, as Steph rolled her eyes and smiled at me.
"Aww," she soothed, patting the side of his leg in support. "Go on, sweetie."
He took a deep breath and looked down at her.
"So, uh, yeah. What was I saying? Being out in LA, we've missed you all, but on the other hand, it's brought us closer together."
Steph peered up at Freddie and smiled before nodding at me in concurrence.
"And being as this is Thanksgiving..."

"There's five days to go yet, buddy," Tim interjected, and everyone hushed him to be quiet, through giggles. Poor Freddie. He looked totally lost up there.
"Thanksgiving is a time for being thankful and grateful for what you have," he continued, before looking down at Steph and holding out his hand. She took it and smiled up at him.
"And I'm thankful for Steph."
The girls 'aah'-ed and the boys pretended to gag, for the most part.
"Shut up, you guys," Steph scolded. "You're ruining our moment!"
"More than you can know," Freddie said with a sigh, closing his eyes before pushing his chair back. Keeping hold of Steph's hand, he lowered himself on bended knee beside her. The table took in a shared gasp of breath and then all was still.
"Oh my God."
Steph was the only one who spoke as Freddie reached into his inside pocket and pulled out a ring box. My eyes were glued to them as he opened the lid and looked up at her with big, hopeful eyes.
"I will never be more in love with anyone than I am right now with you. That's why, and I promise you I've thought this through... Stephanie Hunt, will you marry me?"
Everyone held their breath.
"Yes!" Steph gushed, throwing her arms around his neck and pulling him towards her for a kiss. I gasped, then grinned, then squealed, jumping up from my seat along with everyone else. We all erupted into applause and started whistling and clapping and squealing. I turned to Riley and wide-

eyed him, my hands on his folded arms.
"Can you believe it?!"
"No," he said, letting out a gentle laugh. "I actually can't."
I turned around and watched as Freddie slipped the ring onto Steph's finger and looked at her, smiling. She leaned closer and kissed him again before turning around to face me, jaw hung open, eyes wide.
I beamed at her and pulled her into the tightest of hugs, watching over my shoulder as Freddie was bear hugged by Mattie, and slapped on the arm by a less over-the-top Tim.
"I can't believe it!" Steph said. "We're getting married!"
I looked at her, then at Freddie. This was *fast*. From friendship to relationship to marriage, all in less than a year. But I was happy for them, even if it was a cautious kind of happiness. It was one thing to get engaged, that part was easy, but it was quite another to make it up the aisle. We would have to wait and see how this all panned out. But for now, for tonight, everyone was head over heels for the happy couple.
We toasted them with even more alcohol, the champagne going straight to my head, much to Riley's delight. Eventually, he turned to me.
"I don't mean to cut short this wonderful evening but..."
I nodded at him, pouting my lips to gesture that he should kiss me. He obliged.
"We're leaving!" I announced with a drunken flick of the hand, and Steph frowned.
"Noo..."

We said goodbye to everyone, although I made everyone promise to be around for New Year's Eve for a party at mine that I apparently made up on the spot (again), then let Riley support me as I staggered out of the restaurant. The paparazzi were still waiting for us, and I snuggled into Riley's shoulder as he wrapped his arm protectively around me and steered us to a nearby taxi. Once inside, I repaid my gratitude in a smothering of kisses.

"Hold on there, butterfly," Riley said with a smile. "We've still got ten blocks until we get to mine."

Unfortunately for Riley, those ten blocks sent me to sleep. I remember being helped out of the car and leaning into him as we got into the lift. I think I remember saying something embarrassing like 'Not long now, baby' as he put the key into the door. I *definitely* remember him lifting me up in his arms and carrying me along the corridor, as I nuzzled grateful kisses into his neck. And I know, for a fact, that we didn't sleep together. Instead, he tucked me up in bed and let me sleep until morning. What a gentleman.

***

When I awoke the next morning and opened a bleary eye, I saw a glass of water by the bed and reached for it immediately. Oh, my head...

"Morning, beautiful," Riley slurred sleepily, running his hand across my middle as I lay back on the bed.

"I'm never drinking again," I mumbled.

He laughed gently.

"Yeah, everyone says that."
I turned my head to look at him, his face resting on the pillow. How could he look so good so early in the morning?
"I totally ruined our night," I pouted dejectedly.
"You kind of did," he teased, before squeezing my waist in his hand.
"What an idiot."
"Hey," Riley said. "That's my girlfriend you're talking about."
I smiled and closed my eyes, feeling the warmth of his body lying beside me, the weight of his arm draped across my stomach. I ran my fingers idly up and down his arm.
"I'll make it up to you," I promised.
"I was hoping you'd say that..." Riley drawled in my ear, laying kisses into my neck as he attempted to pull me to face him.
"Just give me an hour to sleep off this hangover."
He paused, mid-smooch.

To his credit, he did. And to mine, I most definitely made it up to him, for the rest of the morning (and a little in the afternoon, too).

DECEMBER 31st

"You've got to be kidding me..."
I glanced up from the schedule and looked across the trailer at Karl.
"Seriously?" Connor whined, and I glanced at him, rubbing his frowning forehead in confusion.
"Yeah, I mean, come on," Josh reasoned. "It's New Year's Eve..."
"Which is exactly why we can't shoot at any other time," Karl explained calmly but firmly.
"So what, we have to celebrate New Year's in character?" Meghan asked.
Karl nodded.
"The writers want you all to go to Times Square to ring in the New Year. It'll be a low-budget, hand-held kind of operation."
"Guerilla film-making," Jared said, with a roll of the eyes.
"Hardly," Karl said. "We're not making a war

movie here."
"Uh, have you ever been to Times Square on New Year's Eve? It *is* a battlefield," Josh stated.
The five of us looked at Karl with an array of disapproving faces. We already gave up so much of our time to the show, it seemed totally unreasonable to ask us to work on the last night - and best party night - of the year.
"And you're sure we can't just like, fake it?" Jared asked. "You know, get some Northeastern students, shoot against a green screen..."
"Yeah, that's a good idea," Meghan agreed.
"What if we shot early, you know?" Connor suggested. "At like, 10pm? Then we could all go on somewhere afterwards and still have a New Year's Eve ourselves?"
We all nodded and started chatting, throwing ideas back and forth.
"No," Karl said, cutting us off with an exasperated sigh. "This is happening, whether you guys like it or not. This is what's in the script, this is what the producers have signed off on... You might be the stars of the show, guys, but you're not calling the shots."
And with that, he bustled his way out of the trailer, leaving us all sitting in stunned silence.
"Well," Connor said finally, "who yanked *his* chain?"
"I know," Josh said with a frown. "What a douchebag."
"He's under pressure," Meghan reasoned. "He's got everyone up top telling him one thing, us to try and convince... Let's not shoot the messenger, guys."

I nodded, looking back down at the schedule. 'Tuesday December 31st, call-time 11:30pm'. Was this for real? Apparently so. How could I not be ringing in the New Year with Riley? Or Evan? Or anyone for that matter? The New Year's Eve party hadn't gone quite as planned, on the account that almost everyone we invited had already agreed to be somewhere else (bad last-minute planning on our part). And having spent Christmas with my family, it had been way too long since I'd last seen Riley. So when he'd asked me to fly over to LA to go to some swanky party at The Beverly Hills Hotel, I immediately said yes. Thankfully Evan also had an invite, to a house party at Eli's back in Philadelphia (which a certain Miss Sadie Simpson was also going to be attending...). So we both had plans we were looking forward to, except now mine had been snatched away at the last minute.
"Excuse me, guys, I need to make a call," I said, getting up and pulling my phone out of my pocket.
"Riley?" Meghan asked, looking up.
I nodded.
"I think we've all got someone to bail out on," Jared said regrettably, and we all split from the trailer to make our unhappy phonecalls.
"Well that sucks," Riley said, after I'd told him about the shoot.
"I know. It's so unfair. I was really looking forward to coming to see you."
"And there's no wiggle room, you know? You couldn't take a later flight... we're three hours behind you guys."
"We're ringing in the New Year in Times Square. Even if I could get a flight at 1am, it would still take

five hours."
Riley sighed at the other end of the line. I felt bad, even though I knew it wasn't my fault.
"Well, I guess there's always next year."
That put a smile back on my face.
"So you think we'll be together this time next year?"
"Don't you?" he returned.
"I hope so."
"You know, sometimes you sound really skeptical about the way things are going between us."
I paused, mid-step, and frowned.
"Do I?"
"You always seem to be questioning how I feel about you. Where this is all going. I'm not a psychic but I'm not a pessimist, either. It's working, isn't it? So I don't see why it won't just keep getting better and better."
I nodded to myself, taking a moment to think. Was I always questioning him? Was I unsure about how serious we could be? Maybe I was still being a little guarded.
"I'm sorry if I come across like that," I eventually replied. "I'm totally happy with how things are between us. And regardless of next year, or the year after that, right now, there's no one else I want to ring the New Year in with than you."
As soon as I said it, I remembered why I'd called him in the first place. I let out a heavy sigh.
"Maybe I can get a red-eye, be in LA early the next morning instead?" I suggested.
"That sounds good. We can have a New Year's breakfast overlooking Long Beach."
I grinned.

"Now *there's* an idea."
"Okay, look, I've got to go. But I'll call you just after midnight to wish you a Happy New Year."
"I guess that will have to do," I mumbled with a pout. "I'm so mad at those guys for doing this to us."
"Go on strike then," Riley said. "What can they do without their cast?"
I paused for a moment, then dismissed it. As *if.* As Karl had put it, this was happening, whether we liked it or not.

***

I looked ahead through the windscreen of the taxi and saw Josh and Jared huddled together with Paolo, the camera guy. I paid the driver a twenty and hopped out, rubbing my hands together in the cold.
"Hey Casey," Josh smiled, before rolling his eyes.
"Jonny, Davey," I replied sardonically, shoving my hands in the pockets of my costume. I was wearing Casey's favourite 'Red Riding Hood' coat, as it was nicknamed, on account of it being a deep red coloured pea coat with a hood. Knee-high brown boots on my feet, with jeans and my own warm woolly jumper underneath, I'd been asked to wear a fake 'Heels University' beanie hat too, to add to the authenticity. I was feeling a little inconspicuous, to say the least.
"Any trouble?" I asked.
"What do you mean?" Jared said.
"Have you been spotted? Harassed for photos...?"
"Thankfully, no," he said, glancing around, "but I

feel a little exposed. I mean, it's just us guys and Paolo."
"What?"
The blood must have drained from my face because Josh smiled and put his hand on my shoulder.
"Don't worry, we'll look after you."
"Are you joking? Tell me you're joking..."
"Hey guys."
We turned to see Meghan coming towards us. Her hair was curled, like Regan's, and she was wearing an army green coat covered in patches, a shoulder bag across her body (again, covered in patches) and ripped jeans with Converses. Regan the peace-loving protester had arrived.
"Can you believe it? They've abandoned us. We're on our own," I flustered at Meghan, who looked panicked.
"What are you talking about?"
"It's just us and Paolo!"
"Seriously? In *that* crowd?" she thumbed over her shoulder.
"You really think there's going to be trouble?" Jared asked, looking concerned.
"We literally look like caricature versions of ourselves," I said, holding out my arms in gesture. "You're telling me no one is going to notice us? All five of us? We'll get mobbed!"
"Uh, guys, I've been told to shoot, no matter what..." Paolo said, leaning in to us awkwardly.
"And shoot you will," Josh said, patting him on the back. "Don't worry, we'll be fine."
"So what's the actual plan?" Meghan asked.
"Well, as soon as Connor arrives, we're going in," Josh said, and we leaned together as if discussing

some secret master plan. "Paolo's going to get some shots of us weaving through the crowd, dancing and stuff, then we've got *our* scene..."
He looked at me and I nodded. Guess which two characters were going to share an unexpected New Year's kiss? It was some sort of cosmic joke. Riley was thousands of miles away, hanging out at some Hollywood party with a bunch of desperate models who would no doubt be flinging themselves at him, and I was going to get crushed to death kissing my ex. Great. Just how I wanted to end 2002.
"Have you seen that crowd? It's insane."
I turned as Connor came up behind me and slammed his hands down on my shoulders.
"This might actually be fun!"
I rolled my eyes and Josh grinned.
"Well, there's no time like the present," he said with a clap of the hands. "Let's go make some television."

***

As we made our way through the crowd, I had a flashback to last year. Instinctively reaching for Josh's hand, he gave it a reassuring squeeze as slowly but surely, we started to get pressed from all sides. People started calling out our real names and I wondered exactly how Paolo thought he was going to get anything he could actually use.
"They're going to dip the sound," he said, as we tried to form a circle with him in the middle. "If they say your real names, it won't matter"
"They'll just play some Cherry Soda over it," Josh interjected.

"Who's actually playing tonight?" Meghan asked me. I shrugged.
"I heard it was Avril Lavigne," Connor leaned in.
"Who's Avril Lavigne?" I asked.
"Oh come on, Beccy, get with the programme."
I shrugged cluelessly at Meghan, who nodded back in agreement.
"Okay guys!" Paolo called over the buzz of the crowd. "Rolling in 5...4...3..."
"Let's look lively, people!" Josh called, jumping up and down. I grinned and whooped, as Meghan raised both her hands in the air and did the same. She put her arm around me and we laughed, trying to look like we were having an amazing time for the camera, the lens of which was just a few inches from our smiling faces. A few minutes later, as some punk-looking girl came out on stage to an enormous roar from the crowd, I figured I might as well try to enjoy myself for real.

***

"Are you having fun?"
I looked up at Josh and arched an eyebrow in response.
"Sure. Being squashed against a bunch of strangers and freezing my butt off is really my idea of a good time."
"Jeez. I was just asking..."
I rolled my eyes and lowered my gaze before glancing up at him again.
"I guess it's pretty cool to be in Times Square."
"I thought it looked pretty wild on TV but being here..."

He let out a wolf-whistle that was lost amongst the din of the crowd and the thumping bassline of the music. A few moments passed and I looked at him, at exactly the same time as he looked at me.
"Listen, I just..."
"Can I say..."
Having interrupted each other, we stopped, paused then smiled.
"You know," he said, turning towards me as a crowd surge pushed us even closer together, "all things aside this year...I'm glad I'm here with you tonight."
As the countdown began, both of us looked over at the big screen.
"10...9...8...7..."
Then we looked back at each other, me looking up at him as he gazed down. This was definitely becoming a moment. He reached his hand up to hold my cheek, the touch of his cold fingers making me wince, as his other arm held strong around my back. I was going nowhere. If I wanted out, I was going to have to seriously make some effort.
"5...4...3..."
Instead, I looked into his eyes for just one more moment before I closed my own and braced myself for the kiss.
"2...1..."
His lips found mine and suddenly, everything else seemed distant. The noise, the bodies, the cold December air - everything became a backdrop for this highly anticipated kiss. I reached up to grab hold of his arm, steadying myself against the back and forth of the motion of the crowd. I couldn't let him stop kissing me. I had to keep him kissing me...

"We got it!"
I opened my eyes at the exact same moment as Josh, and we both turned to Paolo.
"Really?" I asked.
He lowered the camera and pressed some buttons on it, which I figured meant he was checking that he'd pressed record. We waited until he nodded and looked up again.
"Yep, we're all done."
"Yes!" Jared said. "Let's get the hell out of here!"
"I second that," Meghan said, tugging on the scarf around her neck. "I think we picked the most cramped spot in the Square."
Josh looked at me and I looked at him. We shared a smile before turning and pushing our way out of the crowd.
"I didn't think you'd be my New Year's kiss," Josh called in my ear, his hands squeezing both my shoulders.
"I didn't either," I called over my shoulder, reaching up to lay my hands on top of his.
As we finally made it to a clearing, he came to walk beside me.
"But I suppose, in lieu of our other halves, we make for a pretty good stand-in, no...?"
I looked across at Josh, who wore an awkwardly hopeful kind of expression. I smiled back at him before reaching over to slide my arm through his.
"If it was going to be anyone else..."
I faded out but kept my smile. He looked down at me and smiled back.
As the first fireworks exploded above our head, we all stopped to look up at the sky.
"You guys!" Meghan said with a grin. "We haven't

even wished each other a Happy New Year!"
So we quickly gave each other all hugs and kisses, before settling into a semi-circle and, along with everyone else in the Square that night, stood and watched the display illuminating the New York skyline.
Sniffing my cold, red nose in the biting midnight wind, my thoughts turned to Riley, halfway across the country.
"Excuse me," I said, backing away from the group and holding my phone up as explanation. No one really cared and I called Riley, pressing the phone to my ear and bending forwards to try to block out some of the noise.
"Beccy?" came a crackly, muffled answer.
"Yes! Happy New Year!"
"Happy New Year to you too, butterfly," he replied.
"How's it going?" I called into the phone. I could hear music and noisy chatter on the other end of the line… but only just.
"Yeah, good thanks… Hey, stop that."
I heard a girly giggle, I was sure of it. Whoever it was would have to be pretty close to the speaker for me to have heard them.
"Are you still coming in tonight?" Riley asked, distracting me.
"Yeah. My flight is at 3.45am."
"When will you be into LAX?"
"Hopefully by 6am."
"Awesome. Maybe just get a cab to my place, yeah?"
I nodded as I strained my ears to hear his voice. Instead, I heard someone else's.

"Hey Summer, you coming?" some girl called out.
Summer. My heart filled with dread. Why was Summer Delaney, Riley's ex-girlfriend, at the same New Year's Eve party as him?
"Look, baby, I've got to go. But I'll see you in the morning for breakfast, okay?"
"Okay," I replied on auto-pilot, hanging up and staring at the phone. I immediately began to try and reason it away. So Summer Delaney was famous and living in Los Angeles (probably) and the party at The Beverly Hills Hotel would be full of famous people just like her. It was just a coincidence, I told myself. I had absolutely nothing to worry about.
2003 had only just begun and already it was full of drama…

ABOUT THE AUTHOR

C. L. Scott was born and raised in Surrey, England. She studied English and Film Studies at college and later graduated from Roehampton University with a BA in Primary Education, specializing in English. Building upon an avid interest in series fiction, movies and celebrities, the world of Rebecca Russo was created. She has been writing now for over a decade. There are currently 29 folders of stories waiting to be turned into the Diary of an A-Lister series.

Printed in Great Britain
by Amazon